Circles Around The Sun

By J. Douglas Bates

Best Regards

J Douglas Bates

2005

International Standard Book Number 0-974464-50-3
Library of Congress Card Catalog Number 2003111635

In Association with McClanahan Publishing House.

Cover design and book layout by Fishhead Designs.

Manufactured in the United States of America

Circles Around the Sun is a work of historical fiction. While some stories are factual, others have been embellished. Still others are out and out lies. The readers can decide for themselves which are which. In all cases, names have been changed to protect the privacy and integrity of those involved.

All book order correspondence should be addressed to:

Tennessee New Day Press
P.O. Box 249
Cookeville, TN 38503
1-931 260 8181
e-mail: jdougbates@msn.com

We were ring-around-the-rosy children,
They were circles around the sun.
Never give up, never slow down,
Never grow old, never ever die young.

...... James Taylor

Dedication

This book is dedicated with deepest respect and admiration to the men of the Third Herd. In particular, to those who gave all.

Acknowledgments

To Murray and Rachel Cunningham for their friendship and advice. To Dick Campbell for his help and encouragement. And above all, to my wife Debbie, who saw me off,waited patiently and welcomed me home.

Contents

Contents

The Presidio

The country club of the army. The greatest duty station in the world. The Presidio was known by many names, most of them pretty accurate. It sat smack on the beach in San Francisco, near the mouth of San Francisco Bay. The Golden Gate Bridge loomed on the western horizon, and slightly to the east, Alcatraz squatted silently on the surface of the water. Every day, hundreds of ships plied the water, coming and going, disgorging their cargoes of goods. And every day, at the Presidio, loads of wounded arrived from Vietnam. Letterman General Hospital was there and Letterman was the orthopedic center for the army. Letterman was the place they shipped men missing feet, arms and legs. Or those who were paralyzed due to spinal injuries. It was where they sent men who needed serious medicine. And it was where the US Army sent me in October of 1968.

I was a medic, or to be more specific, a 91B20 Hospital Corpsman. I was fresh out of Medical Corpsman School at Fort Sam Houston, Texas, and my new assignment was actually another school. I was supposed to spend the next eighteen months in an advanced nursing school that would essentially make me an LPN. It was good duty. Classes during the day and the famed North Beach at night. Weekends down in Monterey, or just across the bay in Sausalito. Considering where my patients had come from, or where I could be myself, it was a cushy place to spend your time in the army.

On arrival, I was informed that my school wouldn't start for two more months, so I received a duty assignment to occupy my time while I waited. It was beyond doubt, the best job I had during my entire time in the army. I was assigned to an officer's surgical ward. Pre-op: prep for surgery. Post-op: help them recover. Some were older men, retired military in the hospital for anything from back surgery to prostate cancer. But most of my patients were young, junior-grade officers who had lost a limb or two in Vietnam. They were my first real contact with the war, but I didn't learn much from them. They weren't too talkative on the subject. Their conversation usually dealt with lighter fare. There were dozens of these young men who spent time on the ward, but really, just three of them stick out in my mind.

There was Lt. Dix, the West Point graduate who wanted more than anything to stay in the army. His family had been army for several generations and Vietnam was to be his proving ground, his vehicle for promotion, his ticket punch that marked him for high command. These were needful things. Things that were vital to climb the ladder of success in the military. But what was really vital was two good legs and Lt. Dix only had one. His right leg was gone from the knee down. His career was over and he knew it. But day in and day out, he lobbied anybody who would listen to give him the opportunity to prove he could still handle the job of leading men. He received kind consideration, genuine admiration and a Silver Star. What he didn't get was a new command.

Lt. Burns was a bona fide hippie, complete with beads, hair beyond regulation length and an attitude. He was a man in rebellion, the furthest thing from West Point. Yet in spite of all, he was Dix's best friend. He had also left something in Vietnam - his left foot. Burns and Dix shared a room which was a gathering spot for other young officers and the place to be to learn about our Southeast Asian Policy. In the evenings, they'd lay politics aside and go club hopping, usually in the company of some of the young nurses that abounded at Letterman General. One of their favorite ploys was to find a shoe store that was having a two-for-one sale. They'd go in and stage this huge argument over which shoes to buy. In the end, they'd leave an exhausted clerk to clean up a mountain of shoeboxes and walk out with nothing.

When they came in at night, half-lit and mellow, you could sense this chemistry between them. It wasn't overt, nor was it perverted. It was just this thing that existed between these two polar opposites. A kindred thing. It was way beyond politics and far deeper than the surface where most of us live our lives.

Looking back, I know what it was, but at the time I didn't understand. I just thought it was good that they understood each other, because no one else did.

My favorite of all the young guns on the ward was Mister Oliver. He was a WO-1, which was a classification used for warrant officers. Army pilots, especially helicopter pilots are almost always warrant officers, which is different somehow from being a regular officer. Actually, it has been my experience that warrant officers are mainly different because they're weird, which is what anyone would have to be to fly helicopters in Vietnam. Mister Oliver qualified in spades. I mean, he was out there.

When I first arrived at Letterman, Mister Oliver had already been there for two months. His right leg was in a cast from his ankle to his groin. He was in traction and there was a large, stainless steel pin that passed through his cast, his tibia and then out the other side. He spent twenty-four hours a day on his back with his leg slung up in the air and yet, he was constantly hiting on the nurses as if he could get up and go dancing any time he wanted.

Actually, after I'd been there about a month, Mister Oliver did get out of traction, though his leg was still in a cast. I remember coming to work one afternoon and finding Mister Oliver in his bathroom shaving. He had a cane to help him walk and English Leather to help him score. To top it off, he had a date with Lt. Adams, the best looking nurse in the hospital. The mood on the ward that night was quite cheerful as the happy couple left to take a cab uptown. We were all glad to see Mister Oliver get outside again and more than a little happy to be rid of him for a few hours. I should have known -nothing that perfect could last.

I didn't know anything about what happened until I came to work the next afternoon and found Mister Oliver back in bed, back in traction and sporting a black eye. According to Captain Andrews, the head nurse, he was involved in a barroom brawl on North Beach. The story we got was that he had had a few drinks and when a fellow officer made a rather crude remark about the size of Lt. Adam's breasts, Mister Oliver felt compelled to defend her virtue. He took a vicious swing at the other guy's head with his cane. He missed. And in so doing, he lost his balance and ended up on the barroom floor. In the resulting free-for-all, he was trampled and kicked by a variety of drunks and Lt. Adams ended up bringing him home in an ambulance. After emergency surgery, Mister Oliver was back where he started and so was I - servicing his bed pan.

Beyond my ward was a very large hospital filled with maimed men. Some created havoc in the halls, racing their wheelchairs like stainless steel chariots. They turned the corners on one wheel and treated stairways as though they were merely ramps. And these were the lucky ones.

We had several wards filled with quadraplegic patients who couldn't move at all. They were confined to full Spica casts from the neck to the ankles, or they lay like human sandwiches between the canvas layers of a Striker Frame. Every day I walked through the hospital and watched as nurses and orderlies tended to the needs of those men. They turned them over, flipped them from side to side, helped them void, brush their teeth, eat, or even turned the pages of a book for them. I could see the cost of war in terms of human misery, but it was somehow sanitized at that level. The full gravity of being in the wrong place at the wrong time had yet to impact me personally.

With the information I did have, I've never understood why I didn't stay at Letterman General. I can't figure, for the life of me, why in the world I didn't stay for school. Eighteen months in San Francisco versus twelve months in Vietnam should have been a no brainer. But being brainy has never been my strong suit, so one day just before school started, I walked into the school commandant's office and surrendered my student status. I told her I wanted out. No school. Just send me to Vietnam. She did.

My Odyssey

Webster defines an odyssey as, "a long wandering marked by many changes in fortune." That being so, it is the only way to describe my trip from San Francisco to the Mekong Delta of Vietnam. It began on February 26, 1969 when I left the Presidio for Travis Air Force Base, just north of Oakland. All of the men being transferred were loaded onto blue air force buses, which dropped us on the tarmac at Travis. We lined up, were counted and identified, then marched through the driving rain to board a 707 for further transport.

It was a relatively short flight up the coast to McChord Air Force Base, which in turn was only a short bus ride from our embarkation point, Fort Lewis, Washington. Fort Lewis was damp and cold and lonely. Its buildings stood shrouded in a perpetual fog beneath the shadow of Mt. Rainier. It was not a place that made you feel welcome, but that didn't matter. It was only a place of preparation, a place to begin.

First, there was the processing to do. A daily routine of standing in long lines that snaked from one place to another. We moved like cattle, each following the man before him and no one breaking rank. Jungle boots and fatigues were issued in one building, overseas shots in another. Records were checked, destinations verified. It was an endless procession of human misery fueled by utter confusion and the fear of the unknown.

In the evenings, no passes were issued, so there were no trips to town - no way to break the monotony. All we could do was huddle in our poorly heated barracks beneath the glare of naked light bulbs. We lounged on our paper thin mattresses and chain-smoked while men shared stories. No matter that eighty percent of what we heard were lies. We weren't digging for truth, just grasping for entertainment. Early in the evening, almost any topic would get an audience, but invariably, as the night progressed, the topic always turned to women who were fast, cheap and easy. Sexual bravado does wonders for lonely, wary soldiers.

We were in processing for three days and I heard at least a hundred stories, but only one that had any hard evidence to support the claim. It was told by this guy from Mississippi on our final night stateside. He said that on his last night at home, he went to visit an old girlfriend. The problem was, she was now married to another man. Mississippi was right in the middle of a very amorous move when the lady's husband popped in and caught them. The guy then claimed that as he jumped through a window in nothing but his shorts, the husband shot him in the calf of his right leg. To substantiate his claim, the man pulled up his pant leg and proudly showed everyone his fresh wound, complete with entry and exit holes. What can you say to Don Juan with a purple heart?

The morning of March 1st, we boarded another plane at McChord. This one was owned by a civilian contractor who employed pretty stewardesses and soft music. At first, we made the most of the situation, laughing and joking like kids on a pep bus. We flirted with the ladies and pretended that we didn't care where the plane was going. But as the flight progressed, the posturing gradually disappeared and the trip settled into a boring routine. We read books, talked quietly, or slept. Sometime during the night, we developed engine trouble and made an emergency stop on Okinawa. The boy from Mississippi slipped into town to visit the ladies. The rest of us sacked out in some old marine quonset huts.

When I woke up the next morning, I remember walking alone near our barracks thinking about what the ground I was standing on had cost the Marines in 1945. I knew that I was standing on some very expensive real estate. In fact, I once worked for a man who had been involved in the battle for the island. He had been wounded on Okinawa and half his rear end was still there, someplace. No joke. I remember one day at the newspaper office, he just dropped his pants and it was true. The better part of his right buttock was gone. I chuckled when I thought about that day in the circulation department and how all the carriers laughed with Bill about his being a "half-ass."

But then my thoughts took a more serious turn where Bill was concerned. I thought about his wound and then the navy corpsman who treated him, and I remember thinking, "How did he do that? I mean, how did the corpsman do his job? How did he manage to concentrate on Bill, with all that was going on around him?" I'd seen hours of training films that were designed to prepare me for the blood and gore. We'd staged mock battles with live ammo and explosive charges to help prepare us. But really, I knew that nothing the army could do would really prepare me. I wouldn't know how the navy corpsman did his job, until it came time to do mine. And then, I would either take care of business, or not - which was a far more frightening thought.

Later, on the flight line, they lined us up for roll call. Everyone was there except the guy from Mississippi, who never did show up. What did show up, was a flight of B-52's taking off on a mission. I guessed they were headed for Vietnam and I remember thinking how it must be to ride in one of those giant machines. How sterile the war would be from 50,000 feet of altitude. And how nice it would be to finish your bombing run and then return to base to take a shower, eat a steak and maybe catch a movie at the base theater. It had to be a great way to receive combat pay.

When the B-52's cleared the runway, we loaded up and departed Okinawa. I took a seat next to a middle-aged man, who turned out to be an army cook, once retired. "Kids needed dental work and the old lady, too, so I joined up again," he offered. "Besides," he added, "how bad can this be for a cook?"

It was mid-afternoon when our plane began its descent into Cam Ranh Bay. I can still see vividly, the deep blue color of the South China Sea and how the water grew lighter and lighter until it was almost clear when it crashed onto the white-sanded beach. Beyond the shore, I could see the lush, green foliage and the heavy shadows of the jungle. From my vantage point, it looked like a paradise - a place of almost mystical beauty.

Then the wheels touched the runway and everyone on board seemed to tense-up a bit. We spoke in whispers, as if our landing was a secret, and one by one, we filed past the stewardess standing by the door. She smiled. She wished us well. She did the best she could. Then we were through the door, down the ramp and into the most oppressive heat I had ever felt in my life. It felt as though the air itself was searing my lungs.

An officer greeted us at the bottom of the ramp and lined us up on the tarmac. He gave us a short welcoming speech as we baked in the sun. And then, he sent us to brush our teeth. For real. That's the first thing we did in country. The man said that for the next year, we would be drinking water that was un-fluorinated, so, it was critical that we administer a fluoride treatment to ourselves. Each man was issued a toothbrush and a small tube of thick, grainy, red paste. We marched across the runway to a long, low building that looked like a hog shed on my grandfather's farm. And there, beneath the watchful gaze of a dentist, we armed ourselves against the evils of dental disease. Weird.

For the next twelve hours, we moved from one building to another without letup. I spent my first night in Vietnam dragging my gear from one place to another through the sand. The only sleep anyone got was a catnap snatched when the line was held up for some reason. During one of those naps, a siren went off shattering the sullen quiet of our movement. Several men scattered for a nearby bomb shelter, but most of us just lay in a stupor, too tired to care. Besides, there weren't any explosions near us and we didn't know at that point what a mortar round could do to human flesh.

The processing itself was nothing more than an endless series of personal file reviews and lectures. First, they took away all our U.S. currency, even the coins, and in exchange, we were issued Military Payment Certificates - a form of money that looked like it came from Parker Brothers. Then they warned us of the dangers of dealing in the black market. And a doctor told us horror stories about the strange forms of venereal disease that we could encounter.

Our last stop was at the adjutant general's office where an officer reviewed the Geneva Accords with us. He told us what our rights should be if we became prisoners of war. Then he told us that North Vietnam didn't sign, nor did they recognize the Geneva Accords and they would do whatever they pleased with us if we were captured.

The next day, I received orders to report to the 90th Replacement Battalion at Long Binh. Along with fifty other men, I threw my duffle bag aboard some trucks and we made the short trip from the Processing Center out to the flight line where the planes were parked inside steel revetments lined with sandbags. There were no commercial flights in country, just military cargo planes, painted with camouflage. A mixed odor of grease, sweat and aviation fuel greeted our nostrils as we boarded our transport and took our places in the canvas seats, which lined the interior. Things began to change at that point and I think I began to realize that for some time to come, things would be drastically different for me.

Ton Sonute Airbase, our next stop, was radically different from Cam Ranh Bay. There were no white-sanded beaches kissed by tropical waves and no antiseptic cleanliness. There was only miles and miles of red clay, barbed wire and foul odors. Here, the land lay baking in the sun and a constant breeze whipped up clouds of fine, red dust that coated everything. As we waited in the shade of a large, open terminal for transport to Long Binh, I spent the time studying the hundreds of men milling around.

It was the men waiting to leave that caught, and held my attention. There was something different about most of them. Not definable, but easily perceived.

Their uniforms were sun-bleached and torn. Their boots were scuffed and dirty. Their skin was baked to a deep tan. That's what you noticed at first. The surface stuff. The stuff that anybody can see at a glance. But after a while, I noticed something else. It was their eyes. You could sit and look at those guys and their eyes told you everything. There was this bone-deep weariness about them. And this stare that focused on nothing in particular. It was kind of spooky, sitting there in my shiny, new boots and spotless uniform, while these men milled around. And that faraway thing with their eyes, that look. I just couldn't get it, that's all.

I was rescued from my uncomfortable situation when some buses rolled up to take my group to the replacement battalion. Never rode in anything like those buses before. All the windows were covered with heavy, steel screens and the driver had armor plating around his seat. Outside, the scene was one of total squalor. The dusty roadway was lined with little huts built of cast-off tin and ammo boxes. Raw garbage and military refuse littered the landscape and groups of naked, dirty children played in the filth. Barbed wire was strung everywhere and at intervals along the road, sandbagged bunkers bristled with machine guns.

Most of the adults I saw were women, who were dressed in black, silk pants, multi-colored silk tops and cone-shaped straw hats. The few men I saw were dressed in a variety of camouflaged fatigues of one color or another. Everywhere I looked, the hardship and want of war glared at me through unflinching eyes and its putrid odor invaded my nostrils.

The 90th Replacement Battalion turned out to be nothing more than a large group of rundown sheds that stood on a slight rise overlooking the sprawling re-supply base at Long Binh. Everything from the bad food to the cast-off bunks we slept in was coated with a fine, red grit. Aside from the stifling heat, there was this terrible odor that drifted perpetually on the breeze. It almost gagged me at times and I kept thinking, "What in the world causes that odor? Rotten food? Dead animals?" Then, quite by accident, I discovered its source.

I was leaving the latrine one afternoon when the sanitation crew arrived for their daily cleanup of the facilities. Being a medic, I was curious as to how the modern army handled the age, old waste problem. Somehow, I expected some high-tech solution. But I was wrong. The solution was nothing more than a three-foot-long steel hook, a five-gallon can of diesel fuel and a box of matches. The cans were hooked and dragged out from under the benches, diesel fuel was poured in and a match was flipped.

I am quite certain that the putrid odor of burning excrement can never be completely cleansed from the nostrils. It lurks in the deep recesses of the olfactory lobes and like an overbearing mother-in-law, it just waits for the right opportunity to remind you of its presence.

We spent three days at Long Binh awaiting further orders. Three, hot, boring days with nothing to do except sit around and wait. I discovered that waiting was what we did most of the time and that waiting is what a war mostly consists of. I suppose it was the same for the enemy. You just waited. You fought mostly boredom, and the heat and at night, you mostly fought mosquitoes. And you waited.

Each night at Long Binh, firefights broke out on the perimeter where the VC (Viet Cong) probed our defenses. It was my first look at a real shooting war and it was fascinating. I know that sounds odd, but it's true. The crescendo of gunfire would last only a few moments, but during that short interval, the sky would light up with tracer rounds. Red, green and white lines of fire crisscrossed in the night sky while the popping reports of the guns assaulted my ears. If a Cobra gunship came on station, the prolonged buzzing sound of its mini-gun would add to the din and a solid line of fire seemed to float from the snout of its gun down to earth.

From the safety of a mile away, the action had a kind of sinister beauty. In my mind, I knew that somewhere, out on the line, somebody could be dying. But I couldn't connect with that fact. All I could see was the incredible beauty and symmetry of that moment when the sky was on fire and the stars paled in the light of our fury. And I wondered what it was like, to be out there, when the guns were firing and the beauty and symmetry of the moment were lost in the noise and confusion of combat.

Three days of waiting netted me a trip on a small transport plane that took me south of Saigon, into the heart of the Mekong Delta. We flew low and slow and it gave me an opportunity to look out a window where a fifty-caliber machine gun was mounted. I stood beside the gunner and watched the land slide beneath us as the plane moved through a cloudless sky. It was the height of the dry season and the land below lay hard and brown and fallow. Dikes divided the landscape into thousands of checkerboard squares of fertility that awaited the monsoons to bring them to flower. Along the canals and rivers, lines of nipa palms stood lush and green and soothing to the eyes.

An hour after leaving Long Binh, we landed on a narrow, steel-matted runway beside the Mekong River, and the plane jolted to a stop beside a small shed. We were at Dong Tam, headquarters of the 9th Infantry Division and a world away from San Francisco, the North Beach and pretty nurses in starched, white uniforms. As I dragged my duffle bag across to the shed, I glanced across the river at the deep, green jungle beyond and I wondered what awaited me there. It was then that I realized my odyssey wasn't over. It was just beginning.

The Quick and The Dead

"Gentlemen, there are only two kinds of soldiers here in the delta - the quick and the dead." The sergeant paused for a moment to let his words sink in, then he lit up a smoke and continued, "You're here at the Combat Center to learn what separates the two."

Twenty yards in front of us, there was a slight movement and then a canister came tumbling to our feet. There was a low popping sound, then a hiss and the air around us suddenly became filled with purple smoke. The sergeant laughed as we scattered out, then he deftly kicked the smoke grenade away and stood glaring at his new charges.

"OK, look out there!" he pointed. "Where in the hell did that thing come from?" Before us, the earth lay placid, each spot of dust and leaf litter looked the same. The sergeant waited for a moment. No one answered.

He exhaled and watched his smoke dissipate in the still morning air. Then he continued, "If that had been a real situation, out in the bush, chances are most of you would be dead right now. And that funny, little popping sound would have been the last thing on this earth you would ever hear. Think about it."

He needn't have encouraged us too much, because at that moment, thinking about death totally dominated our minds. We were young, we were green and we were scared. But the sergeant knew that, so he softened his tone a little and he resumed. "That grenade came from a spider hole. There are thousands of them out where you're going." He walked out in front of us and kicked back a pile of nipa leaves to expose a shallow depression in the earth where a slender Vietnamese man lay hiding.

"This is Tu. He's my assistant and he's former VC. He knows how they operate, and if you pay attention to us over the next few days, you might just survive." He waited for a comment that didn't materialize, and then he said slowly, "Listen. You don't want to do anything stupid here. The consequences are too severe. Remember, if you're stupid, you're dangerous - to yourself and everybody around you."

The rest of the day was spent learning about booby traps. First, we were shown the most common type encountered - the toe popper. They were simple, inexpensive little devices that could be rigged by the enemy in a minute or two, usually by using our own cast off C-ration cans. They were designed to maim, not kill. A toe popper could remove several toes, or a large chunk of your foot. It just depended on which part of your boot triggered the little monster.

Next, the sergeant showed us the bouncing Betty. It was much larger than the toe popper and extremely deadly. Once triggered by a careless grunt, the betty made a muffled "pop" as it bounced two or three feet into the air. And then the main charge detonated. The man who was unlucky enough to trip a bouncing Betty was allotted just two more steps on planet earth.

There were many more ways to die in Vietnam, and the sergeant was careful to review them all. We were shown hand frags (grenades) with trip wires rigged in a variety of ways and claymore anti-personnel mines, which the VC borrowed from us, along with 105mm and 155mm artillery rounds. Basically, we learned that our enemies were incredibly resourceful, tenacious and fearless. And that they would use anything they could lay their hands on to eliminate us.

The end of the day found us staring into a gaping hole in the earth filled with razor-sharp bamboo stakes. "Men, this is a punji pit," the sergeant began. "Normally, it'll be covered over so you can't see it. And those stakes will be covered with excrement. If you step in this mother, you're in a world of pain. They don't make boots thick enough to stop 'em and your legs will look like a number 10 sieve when they're pulled out. Watch your step."

The sergeant's words haunted me that night as I lay in bed. I kept thinking, "Watch your step," and "Don't do anything stupid." But how can you constantly watch your step and see where you're going? I mean, how could you ever get anywhere? I tried to look at the subject objectively, but I finally decided that there were simply too many days and too many ways to die that stood before me. I also realized that if I was ever going to sleep again, I'd have to change my attitude. And so, like soldiers have done for centuries, I decided that if I just gave up hope, I'd feel better. Then I went to sleep.

At 2 a.m. shortly after I finally dozed off, a siren sounded - red alert. Illumination went up all over Dong Tam and in the distance, I could hear the dull crump of explosions. Everyone in the barracks made for the bunkers that stood outside. We tripped over each other in our haste and pushed the man in front of us to move things along. It was a comical scene - half-naked, barefoot men stumbling blindly in the darkness.

At 3a.m. "all-clear," sounded and we went back to bed. But no one slept.

The second day at the Combat Center was spent moving through an obstacle course of booby traps set up by our friend Tu. We did not do very well and the sergeant wasn't happy. He called us "stupid" and "lazy" and "blind." Then he called us a lot of other things that only army sergeants can come up with and he ended his tapestry of profanity by pronouncing most of us "dead." It was a bad day.

The next day wasn't necessarily better, just different. We were introduced to the new M-16 automatic assault rifle. I'd heard about the weapon, particularly its tendency to jam when clips were overloaded. But I'd only heard about the weapon and seen them briefly since I'd arrived in country. I'd never held one until the sergeant put one in my hands. It was incredibly light. Made of blued steel and black plastic, it weighed a mere eight pounds fully loaded. It looked like a deadly toy.

The sergeant demonstrated how to fire the M-16 and was careful to point out that its light weight caused the weapon to move upward when fired on full automatic. That is, it was difficult to control and would, if not held firmly, end up firing high. However, he also pointed out that accuracy was not the weapon's strong suit. It was its rate of fire. The M-16 could run through an eighteen-round clip in the blink of an eye and it was just the ticket for killing a man inside a hundred yards.

On the fourth day, we learned escape and evasion and the sergeant's opening remarks gave us every reason to pay close attention. "This is the delta gentlemen, and it's a long way to Hanoi. They don't take prisoners down here. They just blow your brains out. So, you need to pay attention to me today because I'm going to teach you how to escape and evade. And rule number one is - don't panic. People who panic do stupid things and that's a guaranteed body bag, if they ever find your body."

We spent the rest of the day learning about the flora and fauna of the delta. We learned what to eat and what to touch. We made floats out of our clothes and learned how to hide from the enemy. The sergeant reviewed Vietnamese customs and told us how to get along with the locals. We had a wealth of knowledge when he finished. It was skill and courage that were in short supply.

On our last day at the Combat Center, we made our final trip through Tu's booby-trapped trail. We actually did pretty good - just missed one. The sergeant seemed pleased and gave us a little congratulatory speech. "You men might be alright, after all," he mused. "Hell, it ain't so bad out there now. Least it ain't Tet of '68. Those were bad times. Gooks everywhere. And the 9th was defending Saigon, fightin' house to house. Now all you got to deal with are some half-starved NVA (North Vietnamese Army) units and a few local VC. If you just watch your step, you'll be OK. Just be quick - not dead."

The Reef

The morning I left Dong Tam, I stopped by to see the sergeant. No particular reason, I just wanted to. He was in his barracks, sitting on a footlocker in his underwear, with a bottle of vodka and some 7-Up. It was only 9a.m. but stress can cause one to drink early and often. I had an hour to kill before my ride to my new unit arrived, so when he invited me to have a drink with him, I sat down. My assignment was to a line company with the 5th Battalion, 60th Infantry, based at a place called Rach Kien. I had no idea where Rach Kien was, didn't have a clue as to what I would be facing, and was nervous and a little scared. I wanted to talk and I needed a drink.

It was kind of odd really. The two of us, I mean. It was a little like sitting on a creek bank with my dad, and while I expressed my doubts and misgivings, he would just nod his head and offer an occasional comment or observation. The only difference was about twelve thousand miles and the bottle of vodka.

At the appointed hour, a supply truck from my new unit skidded to a halt at a road junction near the sergeant's barracks. The sun and the vodka had worked like a sedative - I was fast asleep. A deep voice with a southern drawl woke me up. "Hey, man, you the new Doc?"someone shouted. The next thing I remember was waking up again in the back of the truck and looking out upon the most incredible cornucopia of motorized mayhem I had ever seen in my life.

There were military vehicles of every description. Trucks, jeeps and tracked hardware crowded the roadway, making the scene a sea of olive drab. But interspersed among them and adding splashes of color to the view, were cars, buses, pedicabs and motor scooters in infinite numbers. The Hollywood Freeway had nothing on that ribbon of asphalt. It was a bumper to bumper, endless stream of vehicles, devoid of any apparent regulation. They moved like a school of fish through a reef, swinging this way and that without a visible motive, but always moving onward.

It was Highway 4, the main north-south artery that served the delta of Vietnam and it was open only during daylight hours. After sunset, anything that moved on the road was fair game for our night hunters - helicopters and ambush units.

When the cobwebs began to clear, I took notice of a bus following on our tail. It was a safety man's nightmare. Every seat was filled, the center aisle was packed with people standing and folks were hanging from the bumpers. Cages of live animals were tied to the top and the outbursts of pigs, chickens and ducks added to the general uproar. Along-side the bus and in between every vehicle on the highway were crowded hundreds of tiny, Honda motor scooters, all of them hopelessly overloaded.

The roadside itself constituted another human zoo. It was packed elbow to elbow with every type of vendor imaginable. They squatted on the borders of the dry rice paddies hawking their ware - coke, peanuts, candy, soup and sex at wholesale prices. If they didn't sell it, you didn't need it.

Outside the city of Tan An, we passed a bus that had pulled off the highway for a rest stop and the paddy adjacent to the bus was filled with people relieving themselves. They squatted in little groups, chattering happily and passing around a roll of toilet tissue among themselves with no more thought than folks sharing a newspaper on the subway. I remember making a mental note not to eat any locally grown rice.

A little further north, we got into a traffic jam at the Ben Luc bridge - a bus had broken down in the middle of the span. I looked out over the bridge railing at the wide, brown, rolling river and realized that I was looking at the Mekong River, the mother of the delta. As I studied the stream I had heard so much about, I felt something bounce off the side of the truck. I leaned over just in time to see a red Honda scooter carrying three ARVN's (Army of the Republic of Vietnam) recover their balance and weave on into the traffic. I leaned further over to get a better view and that's when things really changed.

The scooter was trying to squeeze by a new jeep just in front of my truck and it didn't quite manage the maneuver. A side basket on the scooter hit the jeep on the driver's side and it took a lot of paint off as it wobbled by. The three riders on the scooter didn't seem too concerned, but the ARVN captain who was driving the jeep was highly upset. He jumped out of the jeep and screamed something in Vietnamese at the fleeing scooter. He didn't get any response. So he un-holstered a large chrome pistol and started firing away at the fleeing scooter.

I remember thinking, "Is this for real? I mean, do these people really live like this all the time? These people aren't civilized. You don't just whip out a pistol and start shooting because of a minor traffic mishap." It was kind of like a Twilight Zone thing. I mean, you're watching something happen right in front of your eyes and your eyes tell you that it's happening - this is what's going on. But your brain, having been programmed in another world, keeps screaming at you that you're imagining things. No one actually does things like that. That's what it was like.

Miraculously, the ARVN captain didn't hit anybody, the bus was repaired and our trip northward continued. Twenty miles north of Ben Luc, the driver turned off Highway 4 onto a narrow dirt road and slid to a stop in front of a small shop that stood beside the roadway.

"I'm saddle sore, Doc, let's take a little break," he suggested.

We stepped under a thatched veranda that offered shade and as we did so, an attractive Vietnamese woman came out the front door and jumped into the driver's arms. "This is Susie," the driver said in way of an introduction. "She serves the best noodles anywhere in Vietnam." Susie smiled and nodded her head in agreement. She stroked the driver's hair and pinched him on the cheek. Then she jumped down and headed for the kitchen to fix us some food.

In a few minutes, Susie returned with two steaming bowls of Chinese noodles and a couple of ice-cold cokes. I ate slowly, letting the noodles cool on my chopsticks while I watched the traffic out on Highway 4 stream by. But the driver practically inhaled his meal, then disappeared inside with a giggling Susie. During his absence, two small children came out to keep me company and I let them shine my boots for twenty-five cents. On Highway 4, there was always someone who wanted to earn your money, fulfill your needs and welcome you to life along the reef.

Rocky Kilo

The front gate at the Rach Kien firebase stood some hundred yards out from the main perimeter. There was a little shack there, surrounded by sandbags and it had a window where the MP (military policeman) on duty could see the oncoming traffic. The shack stood just a few yards from a Vietnamese school, which had large windows without screens or glass in them. When the supply truck stopped to check in, I looked over the side and right into the classrooms where children sat facing their teachers and a blackboard. Some things are universal, I guess.

While the driver talked with the gate guard, I took the opportunity to check out the place that would be my home for the next year. The ground between the guard shack and the main perimeter had been completely cleared of vegetation. Rolls of concertina wire crisscrossed the open ground and were interspersed with steel stakes holding trip-flares and claymore mines. My eyes followed the detonating wires from the stakes back to large, two-story bunkers, which ringed the compound. At the base of each bunker, the snout of a fifty-caliber machine gun protruded through a slit, and on top of each bunker, behind a row of sandbags, an M-60 machine gun was mounted.

As the truck began rolling slowly forward, I took another glance across the open ground and I noted several Vietnamese burial plots scattered about. The gleaming, white tombstones stood on little elevated mounds and their presence seemed to make it all the more clear that this was a killing ground.

The aid-station for the 5th/60th, was a long, gray building surrounded by sandbags. There was a large red cross painted on the side of the building and a grinning vulture was painted atop the cross. The front screen door opened directly into the treatment room and when I stepped inside, the only occupant was a small, white dog, who lay napping on the concrete floor. Along the painted white walls, ammo boxes containing medical supplies were mounted and the room had a faint medicinal odor.

Centered on the back wall, stood two sets of saw horses with canvas cots stretched between them and nearby, two folding tables held various medical instruments.

As I stood surveying my surroundings, an officer came out of the back room. My duffle bag told him all he needed to know. "You must be the new medic we've been expecting." He offered his hand and introduced himself. "I'm Lt. Morris, the Medical Service Officer around here. Welcome aboard, and by the way - you can just call me L.T. like the rest of these guys. Come on in the back room and I'll introduce you to some of the others."

We entered a small, low-ceilinged room in the rear of the aid-station where several men were sitting around a tiny television, watching the Armed Forces Network out of Saigon. A big man, with an open, friendly face and black-framed glasses was my first acquaintance among the medics. He was Jim Bonner, the ranking medic and a graduate of the 91-Charlie school I had just forgone. Paul Davis was next, a small studious individual who ran the pharmacy and was also a Charlie school grad. There was the medical clerk, John McGraw, who wore horn-rimmed glasses and a serious look. And last of all, there was Sam Waters, a tall, slender, black man from New York City.

While the others continued watching TV, Bonner pulled me aside, gave me a coke and explained the functions of the aid-station to me. There were several of them: (1) We were responsible for the basic medical care of the battalion, which consisted mainly of daily sick calls and treating any injuries that occurred within the firebase. The seriously wounded, who were injured in the field, were normally sent to the 3rd Field Hospital in Saigon. (2) We ran medcaps in the surrounding hamlets where we treated Vietnamese civilians for a variety of complaints and, hopefully, helped to pacify those populations. (3) We ran a daily sick call at the aid-station for civilians who showed up in the afternoon hours. (4) We treated wounded civilians who were brought to us, since local medical facilities were either extremely primitive, or non-existent. (5) We were responsible for VD control within the battalion, treating both the GI's and the prostitutes who served them. (6) We furnished line medics who traveled with the grunts into the field.

Jim told me that the 3rd platoon of Bravo Company had the next medic scheduled to rotate off-line. But they'd left that morning for a three-day operation. "For the next three days, you can hang out here and learn a little medicine," he offered. "And by the way, welcome to Rocky Kilo."

First-Aid

If I had any idea what a medic's life in Vietnam would be like, it was graphically clarified within an hour of my arrival in Rach Kien. My introduction came from a slender, young girl, who never saw me and never knew that I labored with others to save her.

She came through the front door of the aid-station, carried in the arms of an old man who stooped beneath his burden. She looked tiny and frail and blood-soaked. Close on the old man's heels came two old women with their shawls pulled across their faces. They were crying hysterically and trying to communicate in a language that sounded like singing. I was too shocked at the sight of her to do anything at first. So I stood mutely and watched as others sprang into action.

Jim Bonner grabbed the girl from the old man and laid her on one of our stretchers. "I'll go to the ville and get Hue," spat John, as he ran out to get our interpreter. Sam was close at his heels as he ran to find the Battalion Surgeon, Dr. Henderson. That left only me to help Jim and Paul.

They each grabbed a pair of scissors and began cutting away the girl's tattered clothing to expose her wounds. "Hang a bottle of D5W for me!" Paul snapped as he motioned to one of the storage bins on the wall. His command was like a slap in the face and I jumped to work. With shaking hands, I prepared the IV solution and hung the bottle on a wall bracket behind the stretcher. Then, as Jim wiped her bloody body, Paul worked to find a vein that hadn't collapsed, so he could start the IV. I helped as best I could, holding the girl's arm still so Paul could work. I remember so clearly, how her skin felt in my hand. It was soft and smooth like a young child's, but it was cool to the touch. Even with my limited experience, I realized she was in deep shock and the possibility was very real that we would lose her.

Paul's voice jolted me again. "Tape it down. I'll get a quick BP (blood pressure)." He wrapped the blood pressure cuff around her arm and grabbed a stethoscope off the wall. I began taping the IV in place as I listened to the soft hiss of the cuff deflating. Everything was happening at lightning speed, but it seemed like a slow-motion training film. We moved through our procedures frame by frame and each one became forever etched in my brain.

The girl lay quietly before us, staring at the ceiling through blank eyes. Her family stood at the doorway, still jabbering and crying. Jim kept tossing blood-soaked gauze on the floor and across the room, standing atop a chair, L.T. took pictures of the whole catastrophe.

When Jim had finished wiping her clean, I noted a multitude of small holes in the girl's chest and abdomen. Some of them still oozed little drops of life. Then I noticed what appeared to be small pieces of flesh here and there on her body. In an effort to do something productive, I grabbed some sterile 4x4's and tried to wipe the flesh off. They wouldn't move. I guess it was my puzzled expression that caught Paul's attention and he noted what I was trying to do. "She has perforation wounds," he said. "Her abdominal wall has been penetrated. That's her intestines protruding through the shrapnel holes." Then, almost as an afterthought, he added, "She's bleeding like a stuck hog inside. Not much hope here, man."

Paul and Jim had just finished bandaging our patient when Dr. Henderson came in, along with our Vietnamese interpreter. It was not the time or place for introductions, so I stepped away from the stretcher and collapsed in a chair. I leaned my head back and listened numbly as the others went about their work.

Hue interviewed the girl's family. Dr. Henderson, Jim and Paul stood beside the stretcher quietly discussing their options and John was on the field phone requesting a dust-off from Saigon. Everyone was busy, except the white dog, who wandered in out of the back room and came over to lick my hand.

"ETA (estimated time of arrival) on the bird is just about ten minutes," John called from the front office.

Jim motioned for me to join the group by the stretcher and introduced me to Dr. Henderson. He gave me a firm handshake and smiled slightly as he noted, "Hell of a welcome we had for you. You holding up OK?" I nodded weakly to let him know that I was functional and then we moved into position to transfer the girl to the helipad.

With Jim, Paul, Sam and John on the four corners and me walking along holding the IV bottle, we walked down the main street of Rach Kien. The girl's mother followed behind, crying in anguish. Other than a few Vietnamese laundry ladies, no one gave us a second glance. Around there, it was business as usual, nothing to get excited about.

We reached the pad about the same time as the dust-off and when the skids settled onto the concrete, we quickly loaded the girl and her mother. Then the helicopter wheeled away into the sky and we stood watching until it became a speck on the horizon. Only Paul spoke, "She'll be dead before they reach Cholon."

When we got back to the aid-station, Hue told us the old man's story about the incident. "He say they digging new well. Girl hit buried mortar shell with shovel."

Sam smiled and shook his head. "Maybe, maybe not," he offered. "Most likely, they were rigging a little surprise for us and it backfired on 'em." He and the others went back into the TV room, but I needed some time to process what I'd seen. So I sat on a bench in the treatment room and watched as an old Momma San cleaned up the gore.

Sam's assessment really bothered me. I mean, the girl and her family just didn't look evil or dangerous to me. They looked poor and frightened and desperate. Then I thought, "Is that what the enemy looks like? Were they planting a mine?" In the end, I decided it really didn't matter, because either way, the girl would probably die and I would end up in the back room watching TV.

I left Momma San to her work and I went to join the others who were watching the evening news. As I took my seat, Sam jumped up and exclaimed, "It's time for the weather report! Where's L.T.?"

"What's the deal with the weather report?" I asked Jim.

"Bobbi Big Butt," he smirked.

"Bobbi who?" I countered.

"Bobbi Big Butt, my weather woman," said L.T. as he slid into his chair and pulled it closer to the TV.

Meanwhile, the army newsman was turning the program over to a very shapely young woman named Bobbi. Bobbi's hair was very long and very blonde. Her mini-skirt was very short. It was a great combination. When Bobbi reached up with her pointer to trace the highs and lows, she showed a lot more than just the weather fronts.

"I love it when she gives the weather up north," sighed L.T.

In no time, there was a transformation in my own thoughts. The young girl, with her protruding intestines faded from my mind. It was Bobbi that captured my thoughts. She looked soft and pretty and whole. And for my mind, Bobbi was first aid.

The Ville

My first full day in Rach Kien started rather routinely - breakfast in the battalion mess hall then back to the aid-station to help run morning sick call. Stateside most of your patients had internal problems - coughs, colds, upset stomachs. But in Rocky Kilo, things were different. Ninety-five percent of our patients had external injuries of some type. That, or dermatitis in some form, such as ringworm or boils.

The ringworm was almost always between their ankles and their mid-calf, where their boots and socks created a natural incubator for the fungus. As far as the men were concerned, ringworm was a good thing. A really bad case could net them a week or two confined to the firebase. During that time, they had to wear shorts and spend hours every day lying in the sun to dry out. It was good duty - rub a little Tinactin on your ankles, pop some pills, lay out on top of a bunker and dry out. To a grunt, that was infinitely better than being in the bush where life took sudden turns.

For some reason, boils almost always occurred on a man's butt. Treating butt boils was a bummer. You spent hours either pulling the gauze packing out of the boil, or pushing yards of the stuff back in. In either case, it was messy, smelly, disgusting work and by lunchtime I'd had all I wanted of the job. So when Sam asked if I'd go to the ville with him that afternoon, I quickly agreed. Then I asked, "What are we gonna do in the ville?"

"Check the women," Sam replied.

It sounded like a great idea to me, way better than packing boils. So I followed Sam into the back and watched with interest as he began packing a small canvas rucksack with various supplies. First he gathered up some plastic, disposable, vaginal speculums and a large tube of K-Y Jelly. Then he added disposable latex gloves and a flashlight. I was beginning to figure this deal out. Next he grabbed several vials of powdered penicillin, sterile water, 20cc syringes and needles. The picture was getting real clear at that point, so I asked, "Are we doing vaginal VD exams?"

"Well, we're not doing throat cultures," Sam replied.

"I mean, like real, vaginal exams, right?" I asked again.

"Right, that's what we're gonna do. That's my job, man. I go to the ville every other day and check the girls to make sure it's safe for them to work. Ain't no thing. We're doin' the world a service, makin' it safe for democracy and that sort of thing."

So we left for the ville, which as it turned out was no long journey. The village of Rach Kien stood immediately outside our western gate. The main street of the village was maybe a quarter of a mile long and ran on a north-south axis. Along this dusty avenue stood numerous shops, restaurants, houses and public buildings. We didn't go too far from the gate before making our first stop of the day. It was a place called "Harry's."

Sam told me that Harry wasn't actually the guy's real name. He was an American civilian who had married a Vietnamese woman. They ran a neighborhood bar and grille along with a house of ill repute. Harry didn't miss a trick when it came to making money. When we walked in the front door, a cute little lady ran across the room and threw herself in Sam's arms. "Sam, Sam, you number one," she cooed. "I can work now?" she asked.

Sam gave her a hug and sat her in his lap as he slid into his own seat at the bar. "Don't know darlin'. We'll have to check," he smiled. Then he introduced me to Harry and I learned that while we were on the job, we didn't pay for drinks or food. This job was looking really good.

Sam ordered two cold cokes and some fries. "No drinking on the job, only cokes. That's an ironclad rule from Capt. Henderson and I don't push it. I don't want to lose my job. The girls would miss me," he offered. I didn't argue.

After our snack, we went into the back area which had been petitioned off with bamboo curtains and plastic streamers. Inside each of the cubicles was a bed and a girl - pretty much everything the GI's needed. Our first exam was on the girl who had jumped in Sam's arms earlier. Somehow, I expected a little propriety, but there was none and I was the one who was embarrassed. I just wasn't accustomed to that kind of familiarity among strangers.

Sam went through the procedure slowly, taking time to explain each part. As it turned out, she was a good classroom for me because she still had gonorrhea and Sam showed me what it looked like. He also showed me how to mix the penicillin up and had me do the injections in her hips. "Maybe next week," Sam offered as she got dressed and we moved to the next cubicle.

Sam did three demonstrations for me, then on the fourth girl, he turned the routine over to me. I guess I did Ok. I mean, I followed Sam's procedure, the girl was clean and it was over in just a few minutes. My patient said I was the greatest. A number one bouxi (doctor). Sam said I was a natural at it. Whatever.

When we left Harry's, we went to the center of the village where a plaza opened up and numerous stalls formed the Rach Kien market place. I was fascinated. It looked like something out of my 9th grade World Geography book. There were open stalls everywhere and they sold everything you could imagine. There were fruit and vegetable stalls. Several butchers had hung fresh meat. There were jewelry booths filled with gold and a multitude of Seiko watches. Women sold handmade items and bolts of cloth. Men offered hand-forged cookware and utensils. Everywhere I looked, commerce was in action.

In the middle of the row of market stalls, a narrow path turned off between rows of small, stucco-like houses. Sam turned down the path and I followed him on a short walk to the busiest den of iniquity in Rach Kien - the Yellow House. The place was bigger than Harry's and built entirely out of bright yellow tin. It was noisier, had a much longer bar and a lot of working girls. What the place didn't have was a sign that told you where you were. You didn't need one.

When we stepped inside the door, we were greeted by an incredibly beautiful woman dressed in black silk pants and an iridescent red silk blouse. She smiled and kissed Sam on his cheek, then she pinched mine and asked Sam who I was. "New bouxi," he offered. So she flashed a big smile at me and asked what I wanted to drink. As before, we drank only coke and declined anything to eat. We were a little pushed for time and there were a lot of exams to do.

There were three girls who were working the bar only because of infections, so we checked them first. Two were cleared to work and lost no time soliciting customers. I gave the third girl her injection while Sam moved on to start checking the others. We worked a tag-team arrangement until all the girls were checked. Then we moved on and visited three other, smaller operations that were spread out in various locations in the village.

It was close to sunset when we finished up and headed back to the aid-station. On our way, we stopped to get some fruit from a vendor in the market who was just about to close up. As we ate, I mentioned to Sam what a weird day it had been. I mean, I came from a small town in the Bible Belt and what I had seen and done that day.... "Well, let me put it this was," I mused, "I just hope my momma don't find out about this."

We laughed together for a minute, then Sam got a little philosophical. "Look, man, it's just a job. That's all. You can hump the paddies with the grunts. Or, you can hang around the aid-station and deal with things like the little girl yesterday with her guts hanging out. Me, I'd rather spend my time elsewhere. Like here in the ville."

Bravo Company

On the morning of March 17, 1969 I was helping Weird John run the front desk at the aid- station. Regardless of where you are, the paperwork still has to be done. Anyway, about mid-morning, the screen door swung open and a slender sergeant stepped inside. He stood for a moment without speaking and I glanced over at him as I continued with the forms in front of me. It was easy to see he was fresh from the field. His uniform was dusty and wrinkled and his boots were worn out. He wore a sun-bleached jungle hat that was decorated with a rosary woven around the crown, and the cross of the rosary hung below the brim several inches. He was Caucasian, but his skin was a deep, chestnut color, making his pencil-thin mustache almost imperceivable.

He cleared his throat, so I glanced up again. "Name's Scott, Hank Scott. I'm lookin' for the new medic."

"You found him," I countered, as I offered my hand.

A broad grin spread across his face as he offered his hand. "Oh, man," he began, "Man, I thought you'd never get here. Been waitin' for two weeks. Two weeks, hell, I've been lookin' for you more like 6 months! Well, anyways, Lt. Gray sent me to bring you down to Bravo Company. Come on, get your gear and I'll help you settle in. I think you'll like the guys. I mean, they're a good bunch, once you get to know 'em."

I let Jim and Paul know what was up, then Hank and I moved my gear two hundred yards down the road to my new outfit.

The first order of business was to meet the First Sergeant, who was reclining in his office chair when we walked in. He didn't stand up to greet us. He just adjusted his desk fan and proceeded with a canned pep talk. He told me I was joining a good unit. Real hardcore. Then he said that it wasn't that bad in the field and that if I would just keep my head on straight and remember my training, I'd be just fine. I didn't believe him and I don't think he believed it, either. However, in a final gesture of welcome the first shirt pitched me a little cloth goodie bag from the American Red Cross and a green kerchief.

When we left his office, I took the time to read the words embroidered in red on the kerchief. They proclaimed, "Bravo Company - Cong Killers Hardcore."

Our next stop was the officer's hooch, where I met 1st Lt. Donald Gray, platoon leader for the 3rd Platoon of Bravo Company, or the "Third Herd," as he called it. Lt. Gray was young - all of twenty-three years old. He had once possessed a fair complexion, had light blue eyes and blond hair. He seemed genuinely kind, was soft spoken and had an easy manner about him that made me feel relaxed in his presence. He reflected confidence without an air of cockiness and I knew instinctively that I could trust him.

We ran into Sergeant Thomas Boatman after we left Lt. Gray and Hank introduced me to the platoon sergeant for 3rd Platoon, Bravo Company. Sergeant Boatman was also very young. With his smooth complexion and angular jaw, he looked like a Roman warrior. His right sleeve bore the big red one insignia of the 1st Infantry Division, signifying his former unit and Boatman told me that this was his second tour in Vietnam. Like Lt. Gray, Sgt. Boatman struck me as cool and confident. There was this aura about both of them that instilled trust right away. It was like, nothing that happens to us will be beyond our ability to deal with the situation.

We found the rest of the 3rd platoon in the enlisted men's barracks. Their uniforms, boots and equipment lay strewn across the floor, creating a hodge-podge of military hardware. The men, for the most part, lay across their bunks in various stages of un-dress, and the area had the mixed aromas of smoke, sweat and mildew. As we moved down the center aisle, I knew they were sizing me up. After all, in their eyes, I was the new doctor.

Half way down the right side of the barracks, we stopped in front of a little cubicle surrounded by plastic streamers and Hank called out, "Hey, Garcia, the new Doc is here. Can he bunk with you?" There was a muffled reply, the streamers parted, and a chunky Puerto Rican stuck his head out.

"So, you finally got off line, huh, Hank? And this is the new Doc," Garcia mused. He looked me up and down, then, said flatly, "Well, we could do worse." Then he stuck his hand out and a broad grin spread across his open, friendly face. "Name's Ed Garcia, Chicago."

I returned the introduction as I shook his hand, then he and Hank helped me stow my gear in some lockers that formed one wall of the cubicle I would call home for some time. Hank left me at that point, and it was Garcia that introduced me to the rest of the men in the 3rd platoon.

The term, "men," had to be applied rather loosely to the group. They were really only boys cast in a man's role, and not a single person I met that morning could legally vote by the laws on the books at that time. At the grand old age of twenty, I found myself to be older than almost every one of them.

My first introduction was to Gary Coniglio, a nineteen-year-old Italian from New York. Coniglio carried an M-79 grenade launcher, which he was cleaning when we stopped at his bunk. He viewed me rather skeptically for a moment, then he said in an off-hand manner, "Doc, I don't take malaria tablets, so don't bother giving me any. They're bitter. I won't take 'em. Besides, malaria is better than what Simpson caught last week."

I nodded my head and as we moved on, I asked Garcia who Simpson was.

"He was a kid from Arkansas," Garcia explained. "Spect he's back there about now, but he don't know it. He caught an AK round in his head. Hank did what he could, but hey, them things mess you up. Know what I'm saying?"

My next acquaintance was a huge, black man from Philadelphia - Joe McCarthy. He was the platoon M-60 machine gunner and he was stripping the gun down when we walked up. He gave me a casual glance, then he laid the gun aside and gave me his philosophy, "Doc, you just be careful when it gets dark out there. That's always when things happen. Lord, I do hate to see that sun go down!"

Purple Hayes lived in the back corner of the barracks, off to himself. He was the resident hippie of the platoon and when I first met him he wore only a purple headband and a beaded peace necklace. He had a joint stowed behind his ear and a glazed look about him. Purple didn't know I was on the same planet with him until three days later when we went back to the field and he came back to earth.

The introductions continued and one by one, I met all the men of the third herd. There was Johnny Dixon, the platoon RTO (Radio-telephone operator), from the Carolinas; Bob Cole, a Cherokee Indian from Oklahoma; Johnny Clutterbuck, an unadulterated hillbilly from Mississippi; Felipe´ Ramos, the self-appointed point man from Chicago and Charlie Sheppard, a quiet, soft-spoken rifleman.

Their names and faces still visit me in my dreams, and at times, their features are as fresh now as they were then. I can still see Fred Dial's hazel eyes and hear Willie Johnson sing with the voice of an angel. Dave Thomas was cordial, but suspicious of me. Wayne Hawkins had several missing teeth, and when he laughed, the gaps in his gums glared at you.

My last introduction was to Tim Czyzyk, who had a large poster taped to his wall locker that read, "We the unwilling, led by the unqualified, have been called to do the unnecessary for the ungrateful. We have been doing so much, for so long, with so little, we can now do anything with nothing."

With the introductions finished, Garcia and I went back to our cubicle. He lay on his bunk beneath a mosquito net and I sorted through my equipment as a small electric fan gently stirred the plastic streamers. Garcia's wall locker was covered with family photos and as I worked, he introduced me to all his relations. I tossed him my wallet, and he got to meet my family, as well as my fianee´. Garcia was big on families.

Later, the families were put aside and the conversation turned to more serious matters. I asked him about Bravo Company and our commanders. I wanted details on our AO (area of operation). I wanted to know what was really going on out in the bush and what these men I'd met were expecting of me. Most of all, I wanted to know more about a dead man named Simpson.

Garcia tried to put me at ease. He told me that it wasn't too bad in our area and that we were fortunate not to be up north where the troops stayed out for weeks.

"It's too wet down here for long operations," he stated. "We spend a lot of time wading rivers and sloshing through the mud. We don't usually stay out longer than three days, and sometimes, we're just gone for the day. We work mostly from slicks (helicopters). They fly us out, prep the area, drop us off, and then bring us back."

Garcia paused for a moment, as if choosing his words carefully, then he continued. "Look, Doc, when we're in the field, we sleep in a ville during the day. Then, when the sun goes down, we set ambushes and we wait. That's about all we do. We slog the paddies, sweep the nipa lines, look for the VC and we wait."

"Wait for what?" I asked.

"You wait to go back to the world, Doc. To your family. To your Girl." Garcia's eyes flashed as he continued, "You got to get rid of any illusion you might have that we are doing something good here. We ain't. No one on Bravo Company will accomplish anything here. Not you, not me, not anybody. And don't waste any time trying to figure this deal out, 'cause it don't mean nothin'. We're not here to defend democracy, Doc. Hell, we're nothin' but cannon fodder. They send us out there every day to see if somebody will shoot us. That's how they find out where they are. Then they bring in artillery or air strikes and send us back in to pick up the pieces. That's how it works. Listen, Doc, we're here for each other, and that's all there is."

Garcia paused, then he softened his tone and said, "You're a part of the third herd now, Doc. We're family, we take care of each other, because nobody else gives a damn. We work together, we survive. Nothin' flashy, no heroics - just do what we have to. Listen, flashy gets you killed around here - a la David Simpson. You get fancy, get careless - get killed. Not a good idea. Just go with the flow, Doc. And Bravo Company will do the rest."

Field of Fire

"We're going to work an ambush tonight out at Gook Village." Garcia's offhand announcement left me with a cold feeling in the pit of my stomach. I had been with Bravo for three days now and I knew that our stand-down couldn't last forever, but that didn't change the way I felt. I rolled over in my bunk and looked at his face, hoping to get a read on what the night could bring. But there was nothing there - a blank page. So I swung my feet over the side and hopped down to the floor. I tried to make my question sound very casual, like I really didn't care. But that's not what it sounded like when the words tumbled out. "What's Gook Village? What's out there?"

Garcia shrugged his shoulders and exhaled slowly. "Gook Village is in a bad area. We haven't pacified anybody out there, Doc. And when we go in there, they always know we're comin'. They're waitin' for us. So tonight, you be sure you have your aid bag in good shape."

I spent the rest of the morning doing just that. I checked and re-checked my aid bag, counting everything as I sorted through the contents. There were thirty-six assorted bandages, including Vaseline impregnated gauze to treat a sucking chest wound. Two tubes of morphine along with assorted pills for headaches and upset stomachs. Band-aids and antiseptic ointment, water purification tablets and malaria pills which I was supposed to distribute to the men. I had bandage scissors and a scalpel. There were boxes of triangular bandages for making slings and tourniquets. Then I checked the canister of albumin taped to the strap of the aid-bag and I thought I was finished, but I remembered one last item - a package of cards I'd left lying on my footlocker.

The official name of the 3x8-inch cards was, "U.S. Field Medical Card, DD Form 1380." Each card had thirty-two line items that could be filled out to forward information about a casualty. On the front side, everything from their name, rank and service number, to a diagnosis and treatment section was there. Next to their name and service number, the most critical sections on the card for a medic, were numbers 22, 23 and 24. These sections simply said, "Morphine 1st, Morphine 2nd, Morphine 3rd," and there was a little space for a date and time. Regardless of what was going on around you, it was critical that a field medic remembered to mark those spaces, because overdoses can be fatal.

I remember sitting on the footlocker looking at those cards and reviewing what I had learned at Ft. Sam Houston. I looked at the twenty-nine sections on the front of the card and decided which sections mattered and what to let go. I unfolded the small, copper wires that were fixed to one end and actually attached the card to my own shirt at the top buttonhole. Then I took the card off, turned it over and read sections thirty through thirty-two - the sections reserved for a priest or chaplain. On this side, the holy man could record Absolution, Holy Communion and Extreme Unction. I looked at those terms for a long time and I visualized the card attached to the toe of someone I had come to know. I thought about zipping the toe, along with its owner inside a heavy, plastic bag and the little card became very heavy to hold. So I folded the stack neatly, placed them in a zippered, outside pouch on my aid-bag. I turned my mind to other matters.

The M-16 I had been issued by the company supply sergeant was slung from a nail on the wall. I took it down and checked to see that it was clean and well oiled. Then I loaded eighteen rounds of ammo into ten clips and stored the products of my labor in a cloth bandolier that would be worn across my chest. I got my steel helmet off the top of my wall locker and leaned my backpack against the bed. Inside the pack, I placed my rolled-up poncho liner and three meals of C-rations that had been picked from an open case in the middle of the barracks floor. As I stood surveying the pile of things I would carry, I fiddled with the P-38 can opener, which hung from the chain around my neck, along with my dog tags. Then I remembered two other items that were very important- my canteen, which I hung from a

D-ring on my pack frame, and a bottle of mosquito repellent, which I dropped into the cargo pocket of my jungle pants.

There wasn't anything else to do, except wait. So I dozed on my bunk beneath the breeze of Garcia's fan and I thought about what the night could bring. I reminded myself over and over about the three critical things a medic must do: (1) Clear the airway (2) Stop the bleeding (3) Treat for shock. I added a fourth and fifth thing of my own: (4) Stay calm (5) Don't do anything stupid. Remember - the quick and the dead.

Mid-afternoon found us walking out of the firebase and into the village of Rach Kien. When we reached the center of the village, we spread out along the dusty road and sat down to wait for Charlie Company. They had the lead for the night's operation. A few minutes after our halt, Song, our tiger scout and former VC, took a seat beside me. "You bouxi, number one GI," he smiled." No problem, bouxi, Song number one. He take care of you." Then he laughed quietly, turned on his transistor radio and lay back to take a nap.

Half an hour later, the Charlie Rangers came through the west gate of the firebase and moved past us. They were laughing and joking like kids on a school field trip and they stumbled along noisily. When their lead element reached an old iron bridge at the outskirts of the village, they sat down and we all waited for the order to move out.

When the order came, the mood changed abruptly. The laughing and carelessness stopped. We formed a disciplined line of march - three paces between each man, single file and no noise. We left the village, with its smiling inhabitants and moved out into the countryside beyond following a dusty road into the lowering sun. It was hot. My steel helmet soon felt like a twenty-pound weight and my neck began to ache. Dust from the feet of eighty men stirred around me, parching my throat.

Just before sunset, we left the road and turned south into the dry paddies where the rice stubble crunched softly beneath our feet. We walked on the parched earth that was so dry it had cracked open, forming deep fissures that could turn your ankle.

About a mile from the road, we halted briefly while the officers checked their maps. We gulped water from our canteens and we surveyed a small cluster of hooches nestled beneath some nipa palms nearby. There were no signs of life; the place looked deserted.

Coniglio, who was next to me in the line of march, edged a little closer and spoke quietly, "Gook Village, Doc. We're on VC turf here big-time. It'll get ugly after dark." He lit up a smoke and offered one to me. "Better smoke while you can, Doc. 'Cause there ain't gonna be no lights after sundown."

I took the cigarette he held out and lit up my last smoke of the day as Coniglio finished his soliloquy. "Listen, Doc, they know we're here. They knew when we left Rocky Kilo. They're waiting for nightfall and we're waiting for them to sight their mortars in on this spot where we're sitting. Once they've sighted this spot and it gets dark, we'll move a little ways off. That kind of evens the odds. It's kinna like chess, right? You set up one thing to do something else. Trouble comes when we don't move quick enough. That's when it hits the fan." Then he ground out his smoke, pulled his jungle hat down over his eyes and appeared to nod off.

I pulled out my bottle of mosquito repellent and rubbed the smelly fluid on my body to pass the time. The sun dipped below the tree line and the western horizon exploded in shades of purple and orange. The rest of the men dozed silently and I sat nervously watching the village until the darkness swallowed it up. There was no moon that night. An inky blackness settled over us like a blanket.

We moved just after dark into the pure inkiness. No sounds. We just tried to follow the man in front of us and hoped to God, we didn't step on something fatal. I was scared, wet with sweat and had no idea where anybody was. My stomach rolled and a bitter fluid came up in my throat. I swallowed hard and searched in the night for Coniglio, thinking that at any moment, gunfire would erupt. But nothing happened. We moved for about five minutes and settled into our new ambush site. In the village, I heard a pig grunt.

Sergeant Boatman appeared suddenly out of the gloom, walking in a crouch. "You got the third watch, Doc," he whispered. "Get some sack time. I'll wake you up later."

I rolled up in my poncho liner and tried to find a comfortable position amidst the stubble, but found it impossible. It was like trying to sleep on concrete with little nails sticking out of it. So I sat up and stared into the darkness until my eyes hurt. Then I closed them and let my mind wander. I thought about summer nights at home when the whippoorwills sang in the pine woods behind my house. A slight breeze sprang up and I could almost hear the soft whispers of the pine boughs. The next thing I knew, Sergeant Boatman was nudging me gently on the shoulder.

"Just stay by the radio, Doc," he instructed. "If battalion asks for a sit-rep, just answer and say 'Bravo three, situation normal.' I'll be close by if you need me." He crawled a few feet away and curled up. Within minutes, he was snoring softly. Somewhere in front of us, Charlie Company was lying silently in the darkness.

It was toward the end of my watch that the firing started. There was a muffled explosion, a shower of sparks and then the clatter of small-arms firing began. A slow rhythm at first, but quickly building to a crescendo as more of Charlie Company joined in.

In an instant, Sergeant Boatman was beside me. He grabbed the radio and began directing the third herd. "Watch behind us, Doc," he spat. "They may try to flank us!" I hugged the ground and lay peering to our rear. No movement. Overhead, live ammunition zipped through the sky and I suddenly realized that out there in the darkness, someone was trying to kill me. I laid my hand on my M-16 and flipped it off safety. Then I remembered that I had forgotten to put a magazine in it.

I was groping around for my bandolier when Lt. Gray came trotting up. "They've got a squad of VC pinned down on the south side of the ville," he said flatly. "Not much for us to do but lay low and see if they move our way." He looked over at me and asked, "You OK, Doc?"

I nodded mutely in reply, then sat silently watching the action. Red and white tracers crossed in the night like a million fireflies dancing before us. The sinister beauty of what I saw had me spellbound. I couldn't look away.

Then a voice echoed out of the darkness, "Medic! We need a medic over here!"

Lt. Gray looked at me calmly. He didn't speak, but then, he didn't have to. I knew I was about to take an exam, so I grabbed my aid-bag and crawled toward the voice. The hard ground hurt my knees, so I dropped to my belly and low-crawled, pushing the aid-bag in front of me. A stray round passed close by and I halted for a second. My thoughts were jumbled.

The voice rang out with more urgency, "Medic! Medic!" I started moving again, winding my way past the shadows of men.

Fifty yards down the line, I found my patient. It was Purple Hayes. He sat clutching his right hand, rocking slowly back and forth. "Doc, am I glad to see you!" he grimaced.

I expected the worst and visions of gore filled my thoughts. But when I took his wrist and looked at his hand, all I found was a small cut on his index finger. It was an obvious set up, but I was so glad to get the situation behind me, I just put a band-aid on him and crawled away through the field of fire.

Soap

The middle of the day was not the time to be moving around in the delta. Especially during the dry season when the temperature soared above one hundred degrees every day and the countryside lay shimmering before you. Even the winds that stirred the rice stubble were hot and dry, giving you the feeling you were walking in a convection oven. The sun-bleached land appeared almost white and the resulting reflection hurt your eyes and made a pair of sunglasses highly desirable.

What was not desirable was excess weight. But we were going out on a MEDCAP to pacify the population and extra weight was unavoidable. I had four twenty-five-pound bags of lye soap, plus a large supply of pre-packaged pills that needed to be transported five clicks (kilometers) south of the firebase. I didn't want to ask anyone to hump the extra luggage and besides, I was new. So Sergeant Boatman saved me the trouble by volunteering some men for the job.

When he tossed one of the bags to Joe McCarthy, the big gunner looked at me over the rim of his glasses with an icy stare. You'd have thought it was all my idea, the MEDCAP, that is. But I'd never even run a for-real sick call, much less a full-scale medical clinic in the bush. And that's what a MEDCAP was. It was a time when all the sick and infirm could line up for free medical attention compliments of me. Meanwhile, Song would circulate through the village to gather any intelligence he could root out. And finally, at night, we would move into the paddies around the village and try to kill the young and restless who came to visit their relatives after hours. So it was like, at two o'clock, we treated an old lady for a toothache, or her grandson for a cut. At four o'clock we dozed in the shade of her hooch or warmed our C's over her cooking fire. At six we moved into the paddies. And around two o'clock, we killed the old lady's son. Pacify? I don't think so.

Song led the way as our line moved through Rach Kien just before noon. When we crossed the iron bridge I heard a couple of large splashes behind me and McCarthy called out, "Hey, Doc, me and Dial lost our grip on them soap bags. Sorry, man."

I didn't bother to make an answer. How important could two bags of lye soap be, anyway? I just lifted my arm to let Joe know I heard him and I kept walking.

We reached the village about two o'clock and I set up my first MEDCAP out behind the village elder's hooch. Word of our arrival spread quickly and I soon found myself facing a long line of Vietnamese waiting to see the bouxi. For the most part, the problems were easy to diagnose, because the bulk of their problems were caused by poor personal hygiene. The people simply needed some soap and a toothbrush.

It was the tooth problems that were the worst to deal with, especially among the elderly. Almost all the older folks chewed betel nuts prodigiously. The red drool and the odor took some getting used to and I had no dental training. But the locals didn't know that. To them, I was the bouxi, something close to a magician. And I had bonafide miracles in my little boxes of pills.

The children were another matter. Most of them suffered from skin ailments, the bulk of them simple boils. I wasn't equipped to lance boils myself, so I gave them soap and antibiotic ointment and encouraged them to visit the aid-station back at Rach Kien for further treatment.

I felt terribly inadequate to handle the problems of those wretched people. But I soon learned that good intentions went a long way in that land of want. So I smiled a lot and did what I could for them. By sundown, my soap bags and my heart were empty.

When darkness cloaked the delta, we moved out east of the village. We set our 'bush and we waited. But it turned out to be a quiet night; the only movement was the stars through the cloudless sky. I remember leaning back against the paddy dike and gazing upward for a long time. I had no knowledge of the southern hemisphere's celestial bodies, but it didn't matter. I wasn't interested in identification, only in the magnificence of the heavens and the incredible beauty of a sky untainted by artificial light.

The next morning, we straggled back into the village where I rested before my clinic opened. I ended up back at the village elders' place, which was quite nice by local standards. It was twenty by thirty feet of thatched luxury, complete with deluxe dirt floors and a family bomb shelter. The only furnishings were a rickety table in front of their family altar and a couple of hammocks strung from the ceiling beams. A large straw mat served as the family dining table.

The head man spent the morning hours lounging in his hammock while momma-san went about her daily chores. She swept the floor, put some dinner on her cooking fire and bathed the children with some of my soap. Most of the other men who were with me ate their C's and dozed off. But everything around me was new and I was much more curious than sleepy, so I watched with interest as things developed.

It was the children that really caught my attention. A little boy, who I guessed to be about two years old and a little girl, around four, who I supposed was his sister. The boy wore only a ragged shirt that was too small for him and the girl, a pair of silk shorts. They spent the morning playing a game of tag. But the game had a weird twist to it.

The little boy would run around the hooch laughing and squealing while his sister chased him. The weird part came when she caught him. The girl would pin him to the floor and then sit on top of him thumping his genitals while the boy lay perfectly still. Then she would let him up and the chase would begin again.

When it first happened, I thought surely the momma-san would put a stop to the game and scold the children. But she ignored them and went on with her work while the old man lay in his hammock occasionally smiling at me.

Purple Hayes, who was asleep next to me, woke up at one point and watched the children, too. I looked over at him and said, "Can you believe that?"

Purple winked at me, shrugged his shoulders and casually commented, "Ain't no big thing, Doc. She's just trainin' for a job in Saigon." Then he rolled over and went back to sleep.

After lunch, I set up my clinic again beneath the shade of the elder's back porch and the local population started lining up for free pills and a smile. I didn't encounter anything new, just aches and pains. Some of them from the same people I'd treated the day before. It was at the end of the day, just before I closed up shop and headed back into the paddies, that a true heartbreaker showed up.

She was young. Too young to bear the child she carried and the responsibilities that motherhood had thrust upon her. She was frightened. Her baby was in pain. The child's head was covered with boils and his hair was falling out.

At first, I was shocked by what I saw. Then I was angry. How could any mother allow her child to get in this condition?

As I applied ointment to the screaming baby, I calmed myself and asked Song to find out why the girl couldn't take better care of the child. Didn't she at least bathe him on a daily basis?

The answer left a scar on my heart that still exists. "She bathes the baby every day, sir," Song said softly. "But she has no soap."

The Eagle's Beak

The stateside media called it the "Parrot's Beak," due to the way the region looked on a map of Vietnam. But to those of us who frequented the area, it was more aptly called the "Eagle's Beak." One's frame of reference has a profound effect on vocabulary. On March 26th, I made the first of many visits to the canals and elephant grass that were the only physical features of the eagle's beak.

It was mid-morning when we left the firebase and walked out onto the roadway that stretched eastward out of Rach Kien. The helicopters that were to ferry us out weren't on station when we got there, so we laid our gear out beside the road and sat down to wait. Within moments, an old woman and a young girl appeared out of the nearby woods to set up a stand. The old woman started a fire and put on a kettle of water to boil while the young girl began chopping chunks of ice from a straw-covered ice block she carried. They offered cold coke and hot Chinese noodles from their portable kitchen. The food was good and cheap and made the waiting a little easier.

I was only half finished with my snack when I heard the" slapping" sound of chopper blades biting the hot morning air. So I dropped my bowl and ran back to the roadway to saddle up.

It was the first flight of helicopters I had ever seen up close, so I watched carefully as they materialized on the eastern horizon. There were five of them in a staggered line and they came in very low and very fast. On the front of each chopper, a large, white greyhound was prominently displayed.

"It's the Mad Dogs," observed Garcia, who stood beside me. "They're a good bunch to fly with."

When the choppers settled onto the road, they stirred clouds of dust and debris that felt like sandpaper to our exposed skin and I quickly found a use for my green kerchief as I covered my face with it in order to breathe. Out in the paddy, the soup stand duo struggled to hold things down while they covered themselves with their silk shawls.

Everything happened at warp speed. No sooner had the skids of the choppers hit the road, than someone pushed me and within seconds we were loaded up and airborne. The choppers were flying full-bore, nose-down and climbing rapidly into a cloudless sky.

I ended up on the center bench between Lt. Gray and Spider Dixon, the RTO (radio-telephone operator.) Most of the others were sitting in the open doorways with their legs dangling in the slipstream. I remember looking at them, sitting in that exposed position and thinking, "How do you stay in this thing? We're at maybe, three thousand feet, flying along at close to 150 mph. There are no safety belts, no means of visible support. Nothing. But there you sit smiling like a kid on a carnival ride. What's the deal?"

In the midst of my wonder about the flying style of the others, I took some time to look outside, at the ground below. An endless series of dry paddies and small wooded areas streamed by as we flew westward toward Cambodia. Then, a vast plain opened before us, featureless and foreboding. I couldn't figure out how anybody could tell where we were going, or where we were when we got there in that endless sea of grass. But someone had apparently figured it out, because out ahead of our flight, a thin wisp of purple smoke drifted into the sky. It was our LZ (landing zone), and the others around me tensed up noticeably once the smoke was spotted. Beside me, Lt. Gray was busy working the phone, checking in with battalion headquarters. It was almost show time.

When we were directly over the smoke, the choppers rolled over and dove for the earth. I knew that there was no way that the guys on the bottom side of the ship were going to stay inside during that maneuver. But to my surprise, they did and everyone was still onboard when we leveled off a few feet above the reeds, which bent beneath the vortex of the chopper blades.

There was no landing - only a quick hover and we jumped the last few feet to the ground. Then the world exploded around us, as every door gunner in the flight opened up with their M-60's. Bits of broken grass swirled in my face, temporarily blinding me. The air was full of smoke, the smell of gunpowder and live ammunition as the men all around me fired indiscriminately into the chest-high grass surrounding us. Then the choppers soared away, the firing stopped and the LZ became very quiet. My ears rang. My heart was pounding.

Lt. Gray looked at me and laughed. "It's OK, Doc," he remarked. "We're just prepping the area. No return fire. No problem."

I didn't bother to tell him that they didn't mention prepping at the Combat Center.

Within minutes Sergeant Boatman had us formed up on line and we began moving through the reeds, looking for phantoms. The tracer rounds from our guns had started several small fires in the tops of the dry reeds and the wind soon fanned the flames into an inferno. The smoke got thick, parching our throats and blurring our vision. We tried to out-maneuver the flames, but no matter which way we turned, there was only more of the same. Our line of march soon became a trot and then a headlong run as we rushed to escape the fires. There was no order to our movement. We simply ran through the reeds, following the voices of those before us.

Not far from the LZ, we came upon an unexploded 1000 lb. bomb lying half-buried in the soft soil. For a moment or two, we halted and stood gaping at the large iron pod from a relatively safe distance. Then Coniglio voiced the question, which was playing on all our minds. "Say, Lieutenant, can these fires maybe set that thing off?" Lt. Gray wasn't sure of the answer, but in any case, we didn't hang around to find out. One by one, we rushed past the bomb and on into the reeds with Ramos on the point.

A hundred yards from the bomb, our path was blocked by a canal. Ramos stripped off his gear and waded in to check it out. It proved too deep to ford, so a rubber air mattress was inflated and one at a time, we swam the twenty yards across the canal, pushing our gear ahead of us on the float.

As each man emerged from the water on the far side, he quickly brushed off any leeches from his body before they had the opportunity to attach themselves too tightly. They also dropped their pants to make sure none of the leeches had managed to squirm down where they could work unfettered in the soft groin area. It was almost comical to watch as men sprang from the water, slid their gear off the float and then jerked their pants down to expose themselves as they searched quickly for any "hitchhikers."

McCarthy, who had a vocabulary all his own, called them "Thirsty Mothers" and took a kind of sick pleasure in soaking them with lighter fluid before he set them ablaze. "Little torches," he would mutter.

Once across the canal, we moved parallel to it, searching for our enemies' secrets. First squad found a small sampan, which they reduced to splinters with a hand frag. Behind us, the grass fire had burned itself out.

At noon, when the sun reached its zenith, we stopped to rest. We devoured cans of peaches and fruit cocktail while the sun baked us. We drank deeply from the tepid water in our canteens and we told jokes to bolster our spirits. Coniglio found a large leech hiding under the cuff of his pants, which he scraped off and pitched to McCarthy who roasted it.

Lt. Gray told Spider to call battalion with a SITREP (situation report). "But don't mention the sampan," he mused. "They'll only get excited and make us stay here the rest of the day. I don't feel like messin' around out here. No point in it."

Gray was prudent and we thought the better of him for it. He understood the futility of our labor and refused to engage in mindless heroics. But battalion wasn't buying his story that day. They wanted results - a weapons cache or a body count.

So we saddled up and moved further into the reeds, deeper into the beak.

We were tired, covered with soot and soaked with sweat. Maybe we got careless. Maybe we should have tried harder. Maybe it didn't matter. Maybe it was just Ray Lynch's time. I don't know. I only know that Ray stepped on a booby-trapped mortar round and it killed him.

He was walking about fifty yards ahead of me as we followed the trail beside the canal. One minute, he was there walking like the rest of us. Then there was this roar. This incredibly loud roar and Ray flew backward, landing heavily. He never made a sound. There was just this terrible roar and then the sound of debris sprinkling the earth,.

Someone yelled, "Medic! Doc, we need you here!"

I don't know how I got there. I don't remember moving at all. I just remember looking down and there was Lynch's body beneath me on the trail. He made no movement. No sounds. He looked like a marionette with its strings cut. His limbs were twisted and stood at weird angles to his body. Ray's left leg had been sheared at the knee and his blood pooled beneath the stump. His arms were full of gaping holes, as was his belly. A quick look was all I needed to tell me he was dead.

Only his face seemed unharmed. It was smooth and almost serene in appearance. His eyes were closed and there was this sort of peaceful look about his face. Like a kid, taking a nap.

I was in the middle of pulling out bandages when I heard Sergeant Boatman's calming voice. "Save your bandages, Doc. The man don't need 'em. He's perfectly healed, ya know?"

He slipped his pack off and he helped me straighten Ray's body out. Then we spread a poncho on the ground and carefully rolled Ray inside the plastic cocoon.

The other men kept their distance and gazed into the reeds. It was as if not looking made it less real. Less painful.

Lt. Gray rang battalion to request a medavac for Lynch and a lift-out for the rest of us. This time, they didn't argue. For that day, at least, everyone had had enough of the Eagle's Beak.

Wooshes, Whistles and Frogs

There is humor to be found in combat. Sometimes, it's hard to find, but if you really look for it, it's there. Other times, humor is rather apparent, shocking the senses and restoring a kind of balance to a situation that is tragically out of skew. In a war, a humorous occurrence is often just a step or two away from a tragedy. And in those cases, you can only laugh at what happened from the relative safety of another twenty-four hours of life.

April was the peak of the dry season because it wasn't going to get much drier. The monsoons were only a month away. The earth was so parched, huge cracks had opened up and this, along with the rice stubble, gave the land the look of an old man's face

cracked and lined with a day-old beard protruding through a grizzled hide.

At noon, the choppers dropped us in an AO we called Dodge City. The place had a proper name, I'm sure, but to us it was simply one of the many small villages scattered throughout Long Ahn Province - an area south of Saigon, bordered by Cambodia on one side and the South China Sea on the other. We never saw the ocean, but we could smell it if the wind was just right. What we did see was an endless series of rice paddies, nipa lines and villages full of women, children and old men. We never saw any young men, though we did sometimes encounter their carcasses, or hear their screams in the night.

I spent the afternoon in a sort of bored daze. Sprawled beneath the shade of a nipa palm, I let the shadows swallow me up, and I dreamed. I went home. Back to the world, where violence was occasional and death was dignified. Back to a Saturday night at the Redwood Inn, where the burgers were grilling and the music was soothing. Where she waited, soft and smooth, smiling and sensual. Her perfume filled my nostrils and made me dizzy. Her laughter filled my ears and made me smile. Her love drew me away from where I sat and soothed my heart.

When the tropical sky turned to shades of purple and red, we saddled up and left our dreams in the sleepy village. Our equipment had been taped up for silent running. There was no metal clinking and no conversation. Just a muffled motion like someone stirring the bed covers when they roll over in the night.

Out in the darkening land, our enemies were moving, too. Silently jockeying for a position that would give them the advantage. It was Blind Man's Bluff, with deadly consequences.

When we reached our final position, we set our LP's (listening posts) out near the river and settled down to wait. I can still feel the sweat running down my back as I lay on the brick-hard ground and tried to find a comfortable way to sleep. The pungent odor of mosquito repellent wafted on the breeze and the hum of the vicious little bloodsuckers rang in my ears. I dozed off to the regular rhythm of their little wings as they tried in vain to penetrate the poncho liner that covered me.

My sleep was short lived. Delta Company was operating nearby and when they spotted movement, they blew their bush. The flurry of their automatic weapons jarred me awake and I peered out from beneath my poncho liner just in time to see the last of their tracer rounds arc like streams of fire into the blackness. I was still surveying the terrain down river when word was passed to saddle up for a night sweep. The VC were on the run and it was time to spring our trap.

We gathered our gear and formed on line. Then we moved slowly across the paddies, hoping to miss any booby traps that lay in our path. We hadn't gone more than a hundred yards, when Lt. Gray sent word for me to sit tight. He was splitting the platoon into two squads and he wanted me in between the two, able to move in any direction should I be needed.

I was left alone in the darkness with nothing to do but wait until someone needed a medic. At first, I stood fidgeting with my aid-bag, straining my ears for sounds of movement. But then I decided that I might as well get comfortable, so I took my helmet off and sat down on it.

That's when I started hearing this noise - this strange whooshing sound.

"Whoosh! Whoosh!" Like maybe baseballs passing by in the night. I'd never heard anything quite like it. Baseballs. That's what it sounded like - baseballs. Not like an AK round, which sounded sort of like an angry bee. This sound was more of a whoosh.

I cocked my head to get a better listen. No sound. Then it started again, only this time much closer. A cold knot welled up in my stomach as I finally realized that the whoosh was some type of live ammunition and unless there was an immediate change in my position, I was probably going to have breakfast with Jesus.

I glanced out toward the river, where I decided the firing was coming from. When I did, I saw a stream of bright, red meteors that seemed to be coming right at my head. I distinctly remember uttering a loud gasp as I sort of slid backward off my helmet and gulped air. A large dirt clod nearby suddenly ceased to exist. One second it was there and then it exploded into millions of pieces. I envisioned my head suffering the same fate and I lay there completely helpless, like a turtle turned on his back.

Then the firing stopped. No whooshes, no fireballs. Just the steady hum of mosquitos and my own heavy breathing.

Lt. Gray's voice broke through my mental fog. "It's OK, Doc. The navy just got a little confused as to your identity. I've cleared it up now and they're shut down."

"The navy?" I stammered.

"Yeah," Gray explained. "We got a couple of Tango boats helping tonight. You realize you just survived an encounter with a set of dual fifties? That's incredible, Doc. How'd you do that?" He chuckled.

I was too stunned to answer. But glad to accept his invitation to join him and the 1st squad on their sweep.

We hadn't moved very far when a bad night got worse. Garcia, who was on point, spotted some movement. There was a muffled shout and in the next instant, blinding fire as our weapons exploded. Men were cursing and shouting at shadows. In the darkness and confusion, it was hard to tell what was going on around you. It was harder still to use good judgment. You reacted from fear and the desire to live. Above the clatter of our firing, I heard Lt. Gray's steady voice. "There's movement around that hooch. Put some HE (high explosive) in there, Coniglio!"

I heard the "thump" of Coniglio's grenade launcher, but when the round struck the target, there was no explosion - only a cloud of smoke. I watched it rise slowly from the thatched roof and dissipate in the wind. I remember thinking, "What was that?"

The answer wasn't long in coming, because the wind was blowing in our direction. It was CS (tear gas).

My eyes and sweat-soaked body began to burn with a fury. My throat was on fire and it was difficult to breathe. Over to my left, someone shouted, "Gas!" It was a wasted warning, because none of us carried a gas mask. Each man coped as best he could. We hugged the ground and moved forward, trying to work our way out of the stinging vapors.

Out in the distance, Delta Company was still putting out sporadic fire and the navy was cruising the river looking for targets of opportunity. Somewhere, in the dark, the VC were waiting.

All and all, it was a most unnerving way to spend the evening. Staggering around nearly blind, coughing and crying while people shot at you. When the gas cloud finally lifted, I was kneeling in the middle of a paddy, retching my guts out and assuring myself that things couldn't get worse. But they did.

It all started when the boys of Delta re-engaged the enemy. Their FO (forward observer) requested some illumination rounds to make the body count easier. That worked just fine for Delta Company, but for Bravo, it was un-good. The night turned absolutely ugly.

When the illumination rounds started coming in for Delta,

it became very apparent that the artillery battery forgot about Bravo. The huge shells roared like a train as they came over us and then there was a soft "pop" as the flare separated from the casing.

Nothing wrong there, the little parachutes of orange light floated down softly and you could see real good. The problem was the casing that contained the flare. The casings were heavy. Very heavy. And they didn't float down softly. They tumbled end over end from two thousand feet and they made this funny "whistling" sound as they fell all around us. I felt like a slug beneath the feet of a playful child with a salt shaker - no where to go, no where to hide. All you could do was roll up in a tight little ball and cover your ears as the whistling grew louder and the casings fell faster, the closer they got to the earth. The barrage lasted only a few moments, but it seemed like an eternity to me. Surprisingly, no one was injured and what was left of the night passed without incident.

The next morning, we were sitting in the ville eating C's, when Johnny Clutterbuck brought everything into focus for me.

"Doc," he asked, "Have you ever seen a frog smoke?"

For a moment, I looked at him through bleary eyes and then I mumbled, "Clutterbuck, I'm tired. I didn't sleep much last night and we both know that frogs don't smoke. No, frogs can't smoke. Now go harass someone else. OK?"

He ignored my answer. Like a true scientist, he had tested his hypothesis and his findings were conclusive. With a broad, somewhat toothless grin, he reached into the cargo pocket of his pants and took out a large toad.

"Just watch, Doc," he pleaded. "Just you watch."

Clutterbuck took his half-smoked cigarette, stuck it in the toad's mouth and sat him at my feet. To my utter amazement, the toad didn't spit the cigarette out. He couldn't. He just sat there blinking his eyes as wreathes of smoke rolled around his head. Then he tried to hop away, but his gyro was messed up and his legs wouldn't work right . He just sort of wallowed in a circle.

Clutterbuck gave a triumphant smile. Then he pounced on the toad, removed the cigarette and started out the door of the hooch. As he crossed the threshold, he turned back toward me and said, rather seriously, "Remember, Doc, smoking is hazardous to your health."

It was more than I could bear. First, a smile spread across my face. Then the smile became a soft chuckle, which shortly after turned into a belly laugh. I laughed at the smoking frog and at the sorry navy gunner who couldn't hit a sitting duck. Tears of joy formed when I thought about our inept artillery and because tear gas is funny in its own way. I laughed until my eyes were full and my mind was clear.

War is like that - a strange form of life with a vicious twist. And its humor can be sadistic, even deadly. But it's there, you just have to look for it.

Body Count

"Body Count" - the term came into vogue militarily during the Vietnamese Conflict. It did not denote any particular strategy or method of warfare. What it did indicate was the number of soldiers we had eliminated from our adversaries' inventory. To be sure, the average grunt (infantryman) didn't think about it much and we certainly didn't enjoy searching for dead people. But our commanding officers were, by necessity, obsessed with counting bodies, or body parts. It was their only means of measuring success.

Unlike the marines at Iwo Jima, we didn't storm any enemy beaches, scale a mountain and plant Old Glory for all the world to see. What we did, was wander aimlessly from one rice paddy to another, killing and being killed. We counted the enemy dead to see which of us had hurt the other more and at times, the futility and savagery of what we did was more than we could bear.

We often lied to our commanders, staging fake ambushes and calling in enemy casualties that didn't exist. At other times, when we were in contact with the VC, we fired blindly into the jungle and then called in a number selected at random without even bothering to look for enemy dead. Accurate statistics were not our concern, survival was. And each of us dealt with the situation as best we could. One night, I hit the breaking point, where the weight of the madness sent me over the edge - at a place called Ben Phuc.

We were inserted by the Mad Dogs early in the morning and spent the rest of the day lying around the ville waiting for nightfall. Another boring day of waiting. Waiting for darkness to envelope the delta, waiting for the enemy to move, waiting to spring our trap, waiting for death - waiting.

I was leaning against a paddy dike watching the last rays of sunset when Spider Dixon appeared in the twilight. "Lt. Gray says to saddle up, Doc. Time to move," he whispered.

I gathered my gear and we moved off together trotting in a half crouch. When we reached the rest of the third platoon, Lt. Gray crawled over to me and told me to sack out - he wanted me to take the last watch. I smeared some bug juice on my arms and watched Gray disappear into the shadows. A quartering moon bathed the land with its soft light as I curled up in my poncho liner.

It seemed as though I had hardly closed my eyes when someone nudged me and whispered, "We got movement, Doc. Gray wants you at the CP (command post)." It was Sergeant Boatman who woke me.

I pushed my poncho liner back into my pack, grabbed my aid-bag and crawled after Boatman down the paddy dike, where I found Lt. Gray peering through a star-light scope. "NVA unit, Doc. Looks like a full company of 'em. Wanna have a look?" he whispered.

I took the scope and surveyed the terrain out near the Mekong River. In the soft, green glow of the scope, I could clearly see the enemy unit moving silently across the paddies about a quarter-mile away.

"When do we blow the bush?" I asked.

"We don't," he muttered bitterly. "White wants to follow them to their final position, then call in arty (artillery). Maybe a gunship."

Captain White was our new CO (commanding officer). He hadn't been in the delta very long and he was dangerous to be around. White didn't understand that it wasn't a good idea to move around after dark in the delta. After dark, the enemy owned the delta.

We waited for a few minutes to let the NVA get well ahead of us, then we got the order to move out. White was trying a flanking move to trap the enemy. It was for certain a stupid maneuver and very nearly fatal.

Ten minutes after we started moving, when we were crossing some paddies out near the river, the whole world exploded.

The wood line to our right erupted with automatic weapon fire and the air around us seemed full of AK rounds as we sprinted for some near by gravestones that offered cover.

The rest of Bravo Company spread out along the dikes and began to return fire as I lay sprawled in the cemetery watching the tracers cross in the night. Then the mortar rounds began to land among us. It was sickening to lay totally helpless and listen to the mortar round whistle as it arced toward us and landed with a dull "crumping" sound. For the moment, we were pinned down and could only wait

Lt. Gray got on the radio and raised Captain White to get a SITREP. "He's called in arty. Should be here soon. We'll just have to sweat it out for a while," he spat.

Several minutes of heavy firing passed as we leaned against the gravestones. Then, an artillery marking round exploded over the enemy position. "Good mark," noted Lt. Gray. And it was. Within seconds, the HE (high explosives) started coming in, screaming like freight trains in the sky. The jungle was engulfed in smoke and the sound of splintering trees rose above the roar of the explosions.

The hostile fire ceased coming from the wood line, and as suddenly as it had begun, all firing ceased. We lay in a kind of stupor, like we weren't sure if we were still alive. No one spoke. The pop of an illumination round brought us back to reality and we saddled up to sweep the nipa.

I joined the 2nd squad as they moved cautiously toward the trees beneath the artificial light. It was nerve-wracking work, pushing into the thick undergrowth. The pungent odor of exploded shells burned my nostrils and wreaths of smoke still hung heavily in the stagnant air. It was virtually impossible to see much of anything and the fear of booby-traps slowed our advance.

I was maybe thirty yards into the woods, when angry shouting erupted up in front of me. I rushed toward the commotion and broke through the undergrowth into a small clearing where I found several men gathered around an enemy soldier who lay crumpled on the ground.

Redlawski, the first squad leader, was standing over him with his M-16 pointed at the man's head. "I'm gonna blow your brains out, you sorry bastard!" he screamed.

Before I realized what I was doing, I pushed the others aside, grabbed Redlawski's weapon and shoved him back. "Nobody's wastin' anybody," I snapped. "The man's human, ain't he?"

The force of my words surprised even me and Redlawski staggered back beneath the weight of them. "We ought to waste 'i'm, Doc," he stammered. "Yeah, Doc, he's just a lousy gook," someone else added.

"There's been enough waste tonight. No!" I shouted.

There was no further challenge to my position. The rest of the men slumped down sullenly and watched as I began to examine the wounded man.

He was young, maybe twenty at most, and he lay on his back with one leg folded up beneath him. His comrades had stripped him before they fled and he wore only black silk shorts. A chunk of shrapnel had pretty much severed his folded leg and another piece had penetrated his chest. The man was pretty well bled out.

He didn't make a sound. No groans. No whimpers. Nothing. I straightened his leg, applied a tourniquet and bandaged the wound as best I could. I spoke softly to him and looked into his eyes. There was death there. No fear, no pain, no remorse - just death. He was doomed. He knew it and I knew it. The man had seen his last sunrise in the delta.

In spite of the futility of the situation, I did what I could to ease his suffering. I don't know why I didn't just walk away and let Redlawski waste him. His suffering would be over and Captain White would have his body count. But I couldn't do it. Somewhere, from deep within me, mercy rose up and triumphed over judgment. It may sound very noble now, but it wasn't viewed that way that night at Ben Phuc. We were at war and war is a brutal business. Mercy could get you killed in Vietnam.

When I finished bandaging my patient, I covered him with my poncho liner. Then I asked Spider to request a dust-off. His reply was terse and on point. "I'll do it, Doc, but White ain't gonna like it."

He was right. A few moments later the radio broke squelch. It was Captain White. Spider nodded his head in mute agreement with the message. Then, he put down the receiver, looked at me and said, "White's not a happy camper, Doc. There's still an NVA unit in the area, ya know. He's called for the dust-off, but if we get bushed again loadin' up Luke the Gook, it's your ass."

There was a strained silence for a brief period, then Redlawski and several other men came over to join me beside our enemy. "I don't know why you're doin' this, Doc," Redlawski began, "But I do know that if the situation were reversed, they'd have already popped a cap on you. They don't take prisoners, Doc, and they don't show no mercy."

I didn't answer him. I didn't tell him that there would, indeed, be a body count that night. I lit up a Marlboro instead. And as the young man's life ebbed away, I watched my exhaled smoke curl into the night.

Parakeets

There were not many things we could know for sure in Vietnam and only one truism comes to mind: at night, the VC owned the delta. It was his real estate and he gave ground grudgingly. For sure, we could eliminate him. But first we had to find him, and finding the master of disguise in the darkness was no small chore.

One method we used to un-cloak the enemy was the use of highly sensitive listening devices, which we dropped along the trails he used at night. The position of each device was plotted on a map in our intelligence section. When the electronic ears picked up movement, our artillery fired countless rounds of high explosives into the area. Then a platoon of infantry was sent out to assess the damage, or continue contact with the enemy - whichever proved necessary. In either case, it was not very desirable duty.

We called the night flights "parakeets," due to the small number of choppers used. Unlike eagle flights, which utilized five to seven choppers, parakeets used only three. Just enough to carry a platoon of men into the darkness.

On April 29, 1969 the third platoon of Bravo Company drew parakeet duty. The sun hung low over the western horizon when we filed through the eastern gate of Rach Kien, and onto the road that served as our helipad. Three Mad Dog choppers were already squatting silently, waiting for our arrival.

We didn't load up right away. Instead, we stacked our equipment beside them on the road and settled down to wait out the night. If the listening devices were undisturbed, we would sleep along the road bank and our turn would pass quietly. But if something moved out there in the darkness, the parakeet flew. To us, it was a form of Russian Roulette and all we could do was play the odds.

In the fading light, I lay on the ground beside the first chopper and watched with detached interest as the crew chief performed a last minute check on his ship's engine. Meanwhile, a door-gunner went over the two M-60's to make sure they were in working order. Up front, the two pilots dozed in their seats.

It proved to be an unusually clear night and the sky was filled to capacity with brilliantly shining stars. I tried to pick out the Southern Cross as I rubbed mosquito repellent on myself, but my Boy Scout training was only good for the northern hemisphere, so I settled for simply admiring the night sky. Sleep evaded me and I was still wide awake when the whine of cranking engines announced the bad news. Somebody had moved. The artillery battery opened up and the roar of their shells rose above the whirling chopper blades as we loaded up to leave.

It was an incredible flight. For the first few minutes we flew nose-down, at tree-top level, following the roadway. Then we rolled out to the right, gaining altitude as we headed deeper into the delta. There was little conversation as we slid through the sky. I remember sitting in the open doorway with my feet dangling in the slipstream and how the cool, night air pulled at my legs and made goose bumps on my naked forearms. My aid-bag was in my lap and I leaned on it like a pillow while I admired the moonlight that played on the surface of the canals and flooded rice paddies. The land below mesmerized me with its beauty and for a few moments, I forgot that we were warriors. That these chariots of the sky were taking us to a killing ground.

My waking dream was ended when the orange glow of parachute flares came into view and our objective lay below us. The chopper rolled over hard and a cold lump formed in my stomach as we descended rapidly into the LZ. When we neared the ground, the door-gunners began firing furiously as the chopper went nose-up and slowed down. The ship hovered there, about five feet above a flooded paddy and at that point we jumped clear. We landed in thigh-deep mud that was cold and thick. It made any sort of movement almost impossible. To make matters worse, the two choppers following us flew right over, disappearing beyond a wood line.

That left six of us standing almost immobilized about thirty yards from the thick undergrowth where the VC were supposed to be lurking. I looked over at Lt. Gray, who was already on the radio and I yelled, "Who screwed up?" Behind us, our chopper wheeled away into the sky.

Gray shrugged in disgust, then he stated the obvious, "They've dropped us in the wrong place. He's coming back to get us!"

Our ride quickly returned with the door gunners still blazing away. We crouched low to avoid their fire and somehow, managed to slog back and jump on board. The pilot rolled out so low, we barely cleared the treetops. I looked below in the nipa and saw a small cluster of hooches. Several of them were on fire.

We leapfrogged over the village and they dropped us in some paddies beyond where the rest of the third herd waited for us. Then we formed up on line and moved into the trees. An uneasy quietness settled over the area. Smoke from the burning hooches hung thick in the jungle around us and fallen trees littered the area. The pungent odor of burning flesh and nitrite filled our nostrils with the stench of war.

When we reached the edge of the village, I found myself standing beside a hog pen. Inside it, a large sow lay on her side with her young shoats gathered around her. She was dead, split wide open by a piece of shrapnel, but her young didn't know. They were gathered around her, grunting and pushing at her teats. I remember standing there, staring at the pitiful scene for a long time.

Then the sounds of sporadic gunfire broke my trance and I moved on to join the others as we spread out through the village, searching house to house. Other than ourselves, there was no movement among the hooches. The people who lived there had taken shelter inside their mud-brick bunkers and their muffled whimpers echoed through the walls of thatch.

On the perimeter of the village, my fire team came upon a

small hooch with a dead man crumpled in the door way. Fred Dial, who was just in front of me, called back, "Recon by fire!" Then he ran a clip through his M-16, spraying the hooch as he stepped inside to search it. I stood over the dead body, gazing down uncomfortably as I waited for Dial to emerge. Seconds later he came out of the shadows and muttered, "All clear." Then he snapped a new magazine in his weapon and we moved on.

We were approaching the next hooch, when I heard someone yelling for me. "Medic! Hey, Doc!" I left the others and sprinted back toward the center of the village where I ran into Sergeant Boatman. He had an old man and a young boy in tow. The old man was clearly in great pain. He was walking slowly with the boy supporting him and I noticed his right hand was wrapped in a bloody rag.

Boatman pushed the pair at me and said, "Doc, we found these two hiding in a bunker. Take care of them. OK? I gotta get back!" Then he vanished and left me with my patient and the boy.

I sat the old man against the wall of a hooch and unwrapped the rag to expose his hand. It was almost severed. The bleeding had pretty well stopped, but he clearly was going to need more help than I could give him. "Beaucoup Doi! Beaucoup Doi!" (much pain) the old man moaned. I washed his wound with water from my canteen. Then I bandaged him properly, splinted the hand and gave him a drink and two pain pills. There was nothing else I could do for the moment, so the three of us leaned against the hooch and listened to the sounds of the night. The old man moaned. The boy cried softly. I sat in stony silence.

Thirty minutes later, our sweep was completed and Sergeant Boatman came back to gather us up. "You need a dust-off for these two?" he queried. I nodded my head, signaling that I did. Then I draped the old man's good arm over my shoulder and helped him walk out into the open paddies. The boy followed, still crying.

When we reached the fields, I sat the two of them on a dike and lit up a cigarette. The old man nodded at me, so I lit one for him, too, and stuck the rest of the pack in his pocket. You would have thought I had given him a bag of gold. He grinned broadly at me, placed his hands under his chin and bowed deeply in respect.

His gratitude was more than I could bear. Choked with emotion, I started a one-sided conversation with him. "Look, " I began, "I'm sorry about this mess we've made here. I'm sorry we burned your village and I'm sorry about your dead relations and your livestock."

The old man just grinned and bowed again.

I reached out and gently touched his mangled hand and said softly, "I'm sorry about your hand, too. You understand? You bic?"

The old man only grinned and nodded.

We sat smoking silently for a few minutes and then I found myself talking to him again. "Look, this wasn't my idea, ya know? I didn't want to come here tonight and I damn sure don't want to be in Vietnam. I'd much rather be back in the world. Home. Know what I mean?"

The old man nodded.

It was daybreak when the dust-off came in to get the old man and the boy. And on the heels of the dust-off, our ride out arrived. It was a quiet flight going back. I sat in the open door again and took my helmet off so the slipstream could clear out the cobwebs. I stared at the land below me and wished with all my might for some moonbeams to soothe my soul.

The Gods of War

Without a strong, intelligent and trusted leader, a combat unit, regardless of its size, or function, is ineffective. Leadership changes within combat units are unavoidable. Throughout the ages, those who command and those commanded have had to adjust to changes and learn to work together cohesively and effectively. I believe that it can be said, quite truthfully, that a command change is hardest on those commanded. For they are the ones who pay for mistakes with their blood.

Colonel Leonard Grissom became the new commander of the 5th/60th Infantry Battalion in the summer of 1969. During the change of command ceremony, we stood in the searing heat and as the sweat ran down our backs, we listened inattentively while Colonel Grissom introduced himself to us. We didn't care what he said, or how he said it. We would form our opinion of the man when we saw how he acted.

Colonel Grissom was a West Point graduate and he looked every inch of it in his tailored uniform. He wore his soft cap low over his clear, blue eyes and his close-cropped blond hair bristled as he spoke. His boots had a mirror-like shine to them - not a scratch marred their surface. His light complexion showed signs of a slight sunburn and that told us all we needed to know. The colonel had never been in the paddies. He had no first-hand knowledge of field rats, leeches and sleepless nights. Our new commander was here to punch his ticket and earn some combat credit, before he moved on up the career ladder. In short, he was dangerous and it would cost us a lot of lives to help him learn how to fight in the delta.

It didn't take long to see how Colonel Grissom would run things. The changes were far from subtle. During stand-downs, all troops were required to wear full uniforms. No more relaxing in cut-offs out behind the barracks, nor sunning on top of a bunker without your shirt. All haircuts, sideburns and mustaches had to conform to strict military regulations. The colonel and a group of his appointees actually roamed the firebase from time to time to enforce his new policies. It was like stateside duty in a war zone, complete with mindless harassment. We quickly grew to hate the man.

In the field, he was even worse. Colonel Grissom was obsessed with body counts. Not one dead enemy was to go unaccounted for. In a war without objectives, except to kill our adversaries, he wanted to be sure he would be credited with his fair share of the tally. Besides big counts would very likely translate into a star on his shoulder, instead of an eagle. More than anything he wanted to be "General Grissom."

The colonel also changed our tactics to enhance our chances of uncovering enemy units. His favorite ploy was to send a very small element of his troops into areas known to harbor sizable enemy units. Then he waited for the inevitable. The bad guys would let us wander around for a while, maybe discover a small weapons cache or something, and then, at the most advantageous moment, they'd pounce on us and reveal their whereabouts. Once revealed the Colonel could call in air strikes on them or artillery, or both.

Of course, there was one small problem with this mode of operation. Before the jets or high explosives came to bear, we took casualties. Of course, from his command and control helicopter, the colonel saw it as a pretty good trade-off - two or three of us for ten or twenty times that many enemy soldiers. Like Robert MacNamara, Colonel Grissom had bought into the idea that we could win a war of attrition. He figured if we swapped two for two hundred long enough, they'd give up. But the line soldier, the grunt who constituted the "two" in the equation felt that it was bad math. The objective was not worth the price.

Within a month of his arrival, our body count of the enemy soared. And so did our casualty rate. That's when a price was put on Colonel Grissom's head. No one knew for sure who started it, but the rumor was rampant among the men. There would be a five thousand dollar reward paid to anyone who would eliminate him.

It then became a question of time as to who would handle the problem: one of us, or the gods of war.

The situation was brought to a culmination one day out in the Plain of Reeds, in the chest-high elephant grass that stretched forever. We were there searching for a weapons cache that intelligence had learned about. There wasn't supposed to be any enemy of consequence in the area and to our relief, the LZ was cold when we hit it.

But intelligence was wrong. The NVA were there, lying hidden beneath the sea of green. When the helicopters left us and became tiny specks in the eastern sky, we walked right into their trap.

The heavy thud of a Chicom machine gun and the high-pitched pop of the enemy's AK's exploded, as their rounds zipped through the tops of the elephant grass. I lurched forward and lay sprawled in a foot of tepid water, momentarily confused, trying to get my bearings. It seemed like all around me men were screaming and yelling as the enemy gunners took their toll and our guns fired in reply. Smoke billowed in the breeze, making it harder to tell which way was which. Then, above the din, I heard someone call for me, "Medic! Medic! Doc, we need you here!" I was still trying to sort out who was where, when Sergeant Boatman parted the reeds and grabbed my arm, "Follow me, Doc," he shouted, "We're over here!"

I crawled after him, and soon found myself surrounded by casualties. Our point element had taken the brunt of the attack and the toll was heavy. Two were obviously gone already, and three more were badly wounded. I went to work immediately, but didn't get far before Boatman was beside me again. "Make it quick, Doc," he muttered. "We're pullin' back. You can bandage 'em later."

Those who were able, grabbed those who weren't and we moved back fifty yards under the cover of McCarthy's M-60 and fire from the rest of the platoon. We set up a new perimeter and as I began treating the wounded, I heard Lt. Gray on the horn with Colonel Grissom.

"Viper 1, Viper 1, this is Bravo 3. We have many, repeat many enemy, one hundred yards west of purple smoke. We have three wounded, two KIA (killed in action). Need urgent, fire suppression and dust-off! Do you copy?"

Several thousand feet above us, I could hear the colonel's command ship orbiting our position. Like Custer, he rode to the sound of the guns and Lt. Gray nodded as he got the old man's reply. "We got a dust-off on the way, Doc, but first we'll have to wait for a gunship to suppress the gooks. Just hang on and we'll get out of this. OK?"

"I'm alright sir, but two of these guys can't wait long," I replied.

Ten minutes later, two gunships came on station and started making their runs on the enemy positions. Time and again, the cobras would roll out on the reeds with their mini-guns blazing and the force of their rockets exploding numbed my ears. The hostile firing into our perimeter began to fizzle and then stopped altogether.

I looked over my shoulder, and the dust-off was coming in low and fast, with his nose almost touching the grass. When he reached us, there was a quick hover and we slid the dead and dying into the chopper's belly. Then, in a blink, he was gone, gliding swiftly away and clawing for altitude.

I was a nervous wreck and I remember that when I reached into my breast pocket for a smoke, I had trouble getting the pack out. My hand was slick with blood and my nostrils full of the smell of entrails. I just sat down and stared into the sky.

It was at that moment that I noticed the two helicopters above us. One was a cobra gun-ship and the other was the colonel's command ship. Apparently, neither of them was aware of the other. The gunship had gone nose over and was screaming in to empty his ordinance before heading home. The colonel was coming in low to count the enemy dead. I remember following their flight paths and then suddenly realizing that something was terribly wrong.

It was almost like a slow motion movie, yet it happened in a heartbeat. The two ships collided in mid-air. There was a huge, orange fireball and a sickening explosion. Then pieces of people and machines rained from the sky. I remember trying to yell, or scream, or something. But nothing came out of my mouth. Just this loud gasp, as my eyes beheld the fury of the gods of war.

Truck Driver

There were basically two kinds of soldiers in Vietnam, a line- man and those in the rear echelon. If you were on line, you humped the paddies. Your future was uncertain, at best and so you lived from day to day. Mindlessly moving one foot in front of the other, you soldiered with your feet. You slept on the ground, which was hard as a brick in the dry season and during the monsoons, you slept in the mud and water. The heat and the mosquitoes were as much an enemy as the VC and there was no respite from their daily presence in your life.

For a man on line, there were no illusions of victory. We were certainly and painfully aware that there was only one goal on which we could set our sights. To endure. Our only hope was just that. Endure until you got off line, hopefully, with all your organs and various body parts intact. If you could do that, you were considered victorious.

It was war on a very personal level. There was no master plan, nor sweeping strategy, just the movement of your body through the paddies and nipa lines. One foot in front of the other. Each moment more deadly and monotonous than the previous one. And each moment, you became more determined to endure.

The odds were not in your favor. Snipers, mines and ambushes took their toll. Their were twenty men in the third platoon of Bravo company when I became their medic. They were young. At twenty, I was one of the oldest. Of those twenty men, I lost eight dead and five wounded. That's a sixty-five percent casualty rate. Sixty-five percent did not endure.

Almost to a man, everyone in the third platoon wanted off line. We wanted to move to the rear echelon. To be sure, men in the field looked down on those who served in the rear. But we envied them. They slept in a bed every night. They went to EM (enlisted men's) Clubs and had cold beer at night. Many of their jobs were menial and distasteful, but they didn't have a sixty-five percent casualty rate.

Even the lowliest rear echelon man on latrine duty, who spent his days pouring diesel fuel into drums of human waste and flipping in burning matches, had a good chance of going home whole. We wanted his job, not because we were cowards, but because when we measured the risks against the rewards, it just made sense.

Getting off line pervaded our thinking. It dominated our desires. But getting a job in the rear was no mean feat. It required skillful maneuvering mixed with incredible luck. You could shoot yourself in the foot, but that was too obvious, and only those whose situation became desperate resorted to that avenue of escape. You could get hit so many times that your commander figured you used up all your luck, but that was the least desirable method. The odds were too great that the next hit would be fatal.

If you got lucky, you'd come down with ringworm. Then you could rub lots of mosquito repellent into your affected areas and achieve a wonderful rash that would give you a week or two in the firebase to dry out. But that was only temporary.

The quickest way to become a permanent rear echelon troop, was to impress the higher-ups with your ability to soldier. Do something incredibly heroic, or lucky and live to tell about it. That's how Wayne Hawkins became a truck driver.

We were on a night bush, east of Ben Luc. Out where the paddies stretched in endless succession to the South China Sea. Where the land was as flat as a tabletop and the only elevation was furnished by the paddy dikes.

When the sun slipped into the flat-line horizon and the last glow of that huge orange ball shimmered before us, we saddled up and left the sleepy village for our night's work. An eerie quiet settled over the area. The only sounds were the soft clink of military hardware and the crunch of the rice stubble beneath our feet. We walked slowly, timing our movement so that we reached our final position just as darkness closed the day.

Then we set up an "L" shaped perimeter along the dikes, with Wayne and his M-60 at the intersection facing west. Lt. Gray sent Charlie Sheppard and Fred Dial north of us to set up an LP(listening post). Sergeant Boatman ambled along our lines making sure everyone was evenly spaced so that their fields of fire would overlap. There would be no more movement for me, so I settled down to wait in the black void of a moonless night.

I was straining my eyes against the darkness, hoping to see nothing, when the world exploded just after midnight. The heavy chatter of a Hawkins machine gun started first, followed almost immediately by a host of M-16's. Their tracers arced into the blackness like floating fire. In the midst of the melee, a huge explosion shook the ground and then the firing slowed to sporadic spurts.

In two minutes it was all over and for a moment or two, a profound silence settled in. Smoke and the smell of gunpowder drifted by slowly on the warm night breeze. The killing was over, and since no one called for a medic, I lay against the dike and listened to the muffled voices and movements of those who went to check the kills.

The red glow of hand flares soon lit the paddies down where Hawkins and his crew had blown their bush and I watched with interest as their shadowy figures flitted quietly out to check their results. Only Sergeant Boatman had the presence of mind to keep watch in front of us. He sat stoically and stared intently beyond our lines.

Then I heard a soft click as he thumbed his weapon off safety and as I turned toward him, I heard someone approaching in the paddy. Boatman eased into a crouch, took aim and was within a split-second of firing at the silhouette of a man when Charlie Sheppard's smiling face appeared in the gloom.

"Damn, Sheppard! You tryin' to get yourself wasted? I almost popped a cap on you!" Boatman fairly shouted.

Sheppard, relaxed as ever, chuckled at us and said softly, "Someone up here called for more hand flares. I'm just the delivery guy."

"Well, next time you come in from an LP, you make damn sure we know you're comin' in!" spat Boatman.

Charlie was a little incensed at the remark and retorted, "Look Sarge, whoever called for the flares knew I was on my way. Why don't you jump his case? Anyway, here's the flares. OK?" He pressed the flares into Boatman's chest and disappeared back into the night.

Boatman, shaken by the incident, collapsed momentarily on the ground. He took a deep breath, looked at me and said, "This is crazy, Doc. It's getting' too crazy." Then he stood and trotted off down the dike and I was left alone in the darkness to contemplate another miracle.

Ten minutes later, Boatman was back. "We caught 'em cold Doc. We smoked 'em. Four of 'em. One must have been a VC paymaster or tax collector, or somethin'. Anyways, he was carrying a lot of money." He waved a large wad of cash at me, then he folded it up and stuffed it into his breast pocket. We sat quietly for a moment and then, almost as an afterthought, he added, "Bob Cole got five gold teeth and Smitty pocketed a couple of gold rings. Hawkins didn't want nothin'. Anyways, Song booby-trapped the bodies in case anyone tries to move 'em tonight."

Having provided me with the details, Sergeant Boatman curled up to sleep and left me on watch. It was just as well. I couldn't sleep and I needed time to think about what had happened. I spent the next two hours staring into the blackness around me and into the depths of my soul. Somewhere within me, there was a young man who was repulsed by violence and mutilation. But it was becoming harder and harder to find him. He was being replaced by someone else; a new man, cold and uncaring who insulated himself from the softer side of the human soul. I didn't like the new man, but I couldn't do without him. I needed his strength. I feared his power.

At daybreak, the sound of an approaching helicopter woke me up. As I rubbed the sleep from my eyes, I looked up to see the battalion commander's slick (helicopter) wheeling in over the horizon.

It turned out to be quite a day for us. The colonel was overjoyed that we actually had tangible evidence to prove we were winning the war. He actually had an awards ceremony right there in the middle of the paddies, using the four dead VC as a sort of backdrop. Hawkins received a Bronze Star and a field promotion to staff sergeant while the rest of us stood by sleepy-eyed and wet with dew. The battalion photographer was on hand, busily snapping pictures for the division newspaper. Before he left, the colonel offered Wayne a job back at the firebase driving the water truck.

Hawkins was moving to the rear. No more humping the paddies with the third herd and no more ambushes in the night. He had attained the next best thing to a freedom bird headed for the world. The odds had changed in his favor and the rest of us were left envying his luck.

After the colonel left, we settled down to breakfast - C-rations warmed over a C-4 fire. I was sitting on a dike eating a turkey loaf and some pears when Hawkins stopped by for a visit.

"Doc, I've been savin' some special C's for a rainy day. Guess I won't need 'em any more." He opened his pack as he spoke and rummaged through the contents, picking out two canned pound cakes and a spaghetti dinner.

I thanked him for his generosity and invited him to join me for his last meal in the field. "No more C's for you, man," I teased.

He laughed at my remark and sat down beside me. "I ain't eatin' C's this morning, Doc. 'Fact, I may never eat 'em again. I'm so close to home now, I can smell momma's cookin'."

I grinned at his remark, and thus encouraged, he continued speaking, "I've been humpin' these paddies for eight months, Doc. And that's as close as I've ever been to a gook. They was so close, I could smell 'em." He lit a smoke, inhaled deeply, then continued, "I wasn't gonna miss, Doc. I just let that odor get real strong, then I put 'er on shake'n bake. Last night, we got some back, Doc."

I nodded to let him know I understood and then he winked at me as he stood up to walk away.

When breakfast was finished, Redlawski came over and asked to borrow my pocket Nikon that I always carried. I didn't bother to ask him why he needed it, but he shrugged as I handed him the camera and explained anyway.

"I want to get a few shots of the dead gooks for the folks at home. Want me to snap a few extra frames for you?" I shook my head to let him know I wasn't interested and he left at a trot, heading for the bodies about fifty yards away.

Later in the morning, before our lift out, my curiosity got the better of me and I walked out into the paddy where the four dead men lay in a pile. It wasn't what I had expected at all. I stood for some time, alone beside the corpses, gazing at them. Devoid of any human emotion, I carefully surveyed the heap of naked and mutilated flesh. They were all very young, and very dead, if death has degrees. They lay motionless beneath the morning sun and stared into the sky through vacant eyes.

There was no blood. Just a pile of flesh and eyes with no spark of life. I tried, momentarily, to summon feelings of some kind. Anger, or even remorse would have been welcomed. But I could find nothing within me, except questions. "Who were these people? What drove them to hate us? Who would mourn for them?"

I should have asked, "Who will bury them?" Because we left them bloating in the sun when we went to get Wayne his truck.

Short Round

"Incoming!" The shouted warning jarred my senses and seeped through the mental fog of a dog-tired brain. At first, I just rolled over in my bunk and listened for the sound of the incoming rounds. Like most of the men in Bravo Company, I needed to gauge the distance of the explosions in order to determine my response. Unless they were very close, I was staying put. Harassing fire was not going to disturb my rest – I hadn't seen a bed for a week.

The first sergeant burst into the barracks wearing only his pants and a flak jacket. "Let's go, Bravo! We got movement out on the wire and Chuck(VC) is puttin' rockets in our pockets! North Perimeter - now move it!"

We moved, but with great reluctance. There wasn't any small arms fire to be heard and out on the berm, the bunkers were quiet.

"Top takes this whole thing too serious," muttered Garcia as he rolled out of his lower bunk and pulled on his pants. "If we got movement, why ain't the berm lit up? And how come I don't hear Charlie Company movin' around? Movement my butt, only thing movin' is Top and he's too easy to get stirred up. Come on, Doc. Let's get out to the wire before we're invaded."

I jerked on a pair of pants myself, grabbed my aid-bag and followed Ed out the back door, where we both nearly tripped over Purple Hayes, who had passed out on the back steps earlier. We tried to roust him, but Purple was in no condition to do anything. He'd been to the ville and bought some of the head man's private stock of marijuana. Purple was wasted.

Ed and I followed the rest of Bravo Company across the plank bridge that spanned our blooper pond and made a fifty-yard dash for the wire. Off to our left, a few mortar rounds landed in the open ground. The artillery battery out behind the aid-station cranked up and began firing, a siren sounded and the sky above.

the firebase began to fill with parachute flares. Beyond the wire, everything was quiet.

More mortar rounds landed and the Delta Company shower house caved in. The men atop a nearby bunker hooted and laughed about the situation. It was the Fourth of July and New Year's Day all rolled into one with the VC supplying the fireworks. At that point anyway, nothing of consequence had been destroyed.

Purple Hayes wandered into our position, naked and carrying an unloaded M-16. He pointed to the sky and said, "Everyone smiles as you drift by the flowers that grow so incredibly high!"

We all laughed at him and then joined in to sing the chorus, "Lucy in the sky with diamonds!" Since we couldn't make it to Woodstock, we had our own festival.

Out behind our position, between the wire and the main compound, the Bravo Company mortar platoon began returning fire. They had no particular target, but any time we had incoming rounds, they fired on grid coordinates that were suspected enemy staging points. You could hear the mortar sergeant calling cadence. "Hang!" then a second later, "Fire!"

There was a heavy, muffled thump, as the 4.2-inch mortar propelled its high explosive into the air and then a satisfying whistle, as the round arched away from us into the darkness.

There was a slight lull in the action and Lt. Gray moved along our line checking on us. "Great way to spend a stand-down," he offered. Then he spied Purple Hayes dozing nearby. "Doc, is Purple stoned?" he asked.

"I don't know, sir," I began, "But I do know he can't hurt anybody. His 16 is empty."

Gray looked at Hayes for a moment, then back at me. "Doc, you look after him. OK? And don't let Top, or Captain White, see him either. You copy?" He turned to leave, then he stopped and looked back at me. "And tell Purple, when he comes down, if I ever catch him smokin' dope in the bush, I'll personally beat him senseless."

Lt. Gray hadn't been gone for more than a minute when a tripflare went up from the area out in front of us. The .50 caliber machine gun in a nearby bunker cut loose immediately, its heavy thuds shaking the ground beneath us. Someone blew a claymore and several men began firing indiscriminately.

It lasted all of two minutes and then it was over. Beyond the wire, it was still quiet, no movement. Flares went up again and a squad was sent out to sweep the area. When they came back in, they were barking.

"We just wasted Deputy Dawg," smirked the squad leader.

Spider rang up battalion and reported, "We got one VC out here. That's V, as in vicious and C, as in canine. He was inside the wire, but he's wasted now."

There was a slight pause, and then I could hear someone on the other end of the net yelling obscenities into the phone. When Spider signed off, he looked at me and said, "Ya know, Doc, Major Hansen has absolutely no sense of humor."

The lull in the incoming rounds ended and several more landed near the motor pool. That's when our mortar platoon cranked back up and I guess it was on the third, or fourth round they fired that something went wrong. I heard the mortar sergeant, calling cadence like before, but that third or fourth round sounded different when it left the tube. I remember I looked at Ed, as if to say, "That don't sound too good." And then the shell shot into the sky. Not out, like the others; it sounded like the thing just went straight up and then turned and began falling back to earth.

Actually, it didn't fall straight down. The shell made about a three-hundred-yard arc and landed on the Yellow House, the most revered house of light pleasure in the village of Rach Kien. There was this huge explosion and pieces of yellow tin began raining from the sky. A prolonged groan went up, as hundreds of men watched their happy memories disintegrate before their eyes. It was a tragedy of epic proportions, never to be forgotten by those who witnessed it.

There was no danger to human life. The place was closed up after sundown. But the Yellow House was gone, replaced by a huge crater and a pall of smoke. We felt like a bunch of orphans watching our playground disappear under asphalt. It was demoralizing.

After the short round, all firing stopped. Even the gooks called it quits. I gathered up Purple Hayes and Ed helped me carry him back toward the barracks, past the blooper pond and our mortar pit, where a fight had broken out. It seems there was some disagreement as to who was responsible for the short round.

Charlie

There was nothing dignified, nor comforting about Charlie Sheppard's death. It was not a welcome release from the world he knew. It was not a sacrifice for a worthy cause. Charlie's death was senseless and without purpose. He went through a portal into another dimension thrashing and screaming. His face reflected absolute terror, and whether he experienced rage or regret, only he knew. All I know for sure, is that he died in agony and I live with the pain of losing him.

Sometimes Charlie appears in my dreams. But not as he looked in those final moments. He always looks young and handsome and happy to be alive. He still has that easy laugh that made you feel comfortable and that calm, reliable way about him. In combat, Charlie was all business, never careless, never foolish. Just rock steady. You'd never know, to look at him, that he had a broken heart.

When Charlie left the south side of Chicago to go to Vietnam, his wife divorced him. The loss of her love and his young daughter were more painful than he cared to admit. He carried their pictures in his wallet, which he carefully wrapped in plastic and buttoned in his breast pocket. Every night, when we were in the field, I watched Charlie take the plastic pouch, unwrap it and look at those pictures.

Maybe part of the pain of losing Charlie was because we weren't supposed to be in any real danger. Our platoon was supposed to be on the gravy train as a reward for some recent heavy action. We were just sitting on a huge, ocean-going sand dredge in the middle of the Mekong River. The dredge's job was to pump sand through a pipeline to the local navy base. Our job was to pull security on the dredge at night. During the day, we read books, played cards or swam in the river. At night, we tossed explosive charges into the water to discourage VC swimmers from attaching a charge to the dredge. It was supposed to be easy duty.

The navy base sent three hot meals a day down river to us. The dredge had a real flush toilet and a hot shower. These commodities were in short supply for us. We hadn't seen any of them in three months. What we had seen was unbearable heat, booby traps and death that occurred in a blinding flash of orange flame. No time to react. You either died, or you didn't.

It was on the third night that Charlie died. We played acey-deucey until nearly midnight. Then we all stood by the ship's rail and watched a 40mm automatic cannon from the navy base performing a firing mission. The "pom,pom,pom" sound of the gun and the brilliant stream of red fire arcing across the sky made great entertainment. Never mind, that on the receiving end of that situation, people were experiencing hell on earth. People were dying. To us, it was like a trip to Disneyland. Really weird.

When the light show was over, everyone turned in except the guys who were standing watch, lobbing explosives. Charlie had the bow watch. As I made my way to the CP tent, I saw him sitting under a spotlight with his wallet in his lap. And I dozed off to the sound of muffled explosions from the charges Charlie was throwing. Like outgoing artillery, they posed no threat to me and I rested comfortably.

In the early morning hours, a rough shove on my shoulder and an urgent voice ended my sleep. "Get up, Doc! Saddle up! It's Charlie and he's hurt bad!" Sergeant Boatman's word's jarred me awake. I grabbed my aid-bag and ran after him in nothing but the cut-off shorts I was sleeping in.

When I reached Charlie, one glance told me that "Hurt bad," was not anywhere close to describing his condition. Apparently, one of his C-4 charges had exploded prematurely. He was thrashing around in a pool of blood, screaming and moaning. His right arm was gone below the elbow. His entire chest and abdomen area had been opened up like a ripe watermelon. I knew Charlie wouldn't survive.

When I knelt down over him and began to work, he stopped thrashing and began to mutter only soft, guttural sounds.

"It's OK, Charlie, you're gonna be alright. Just take it easy." I spoke the words gently and confidently because that's what I'd been trained to do. But I was lying and Charlie knew it. When I looked into his face, into his eyes, I saw death looking back at me.

A voice in my brain said, "Ease his pain and let him go." But my heart said, "Don't you give up! Don't ever give up!"

I finished my work and we loaded Charlie on a stretcher to await evacuation. Then we got some more bad news.

"They can't bring a slick in here, Doc. We gotta take Charlie down to the navy base." It was Spider who brought the message.

A navy Tango boat was tied up alongside the dredge, so we loaded Charlie on board for the trip down-river. Sergeant Boatman volunteered to come along and I was glad for the company. As the boat eased into the current, I tucked a poncho liner tightly around Charlie to keep him warm. Then I unwrapped my Albumin and tried to start an IV. But his veins had collapsed - no go. I checked his pulse. It was so weak, it was almost undetectable. He was slipping into deep shock. I started CPR and Sergeant Boatman talked to God.

About a mile west of the dredge, Charlie's struggle ended. He passed quietly, almost peacefully. I remember the feeling of utter futility that flooded over me when I realized that there wasn't anything else I could do. I kicked the bottle of Albumin over the side of the boat. I looked at Boatman and he read my glance, but I heard myself speak the words anyway, "He's gone," I whispered.

Boatman grabbed Charlie by the shoulders. He shook him violently and he yelled at the corpse, "Don't die, Charlie! Damn-it, you can't die on us! You can't!"

I reached out and touched Boatman gently on the shoulder. I remember distinctly the sound that came from him next. It was a cross between a gasp and a moan. As if he didn't know which emotion was in control. Then he leaned back against the wheel house and simply stared into the sky.

There was nothing left for me to do for Charlie except to

close his eyes for him. I did that very gently and covered his face with the poncho liner. Then I told him that I was sorry that I couldn't save him. I held his lifeless hand. I listened to the sound of the water slapping the boat's hull. And I said a prayer for Charlie.

Tides

It was the middle of the afternoon when the three choppers lifted off the helipad at Rach Kien and flew south into a driving rain. We sat in the open doorways with our feet dangling toward the earth and watched as the land disappeared into the cloudbanks beneath us. Everyone was already soaked to the skin and the certain knowledge that we would remain in that condition for the next twenty-four hours did nothing to comfort us. When we reached altitude and the choppers were flying flat-out, the wind rushed across our exposed bodies, chilling us to the bone.

In the midst of such misery, my mind reached for any shred of hope that things would improve. That the rain would stop – no chance, it was the monsoons. That the choppers would turn around and the mission would be scrubbed – not likely, hadn't happened yet. That you would find a warm, dry place for the night – "Neva happen GI."

When hopelessness overwhelms, the mind free-falls. You go numb. I closed my eyes and listened to the steady chop of the blades biting into the sky and let the vibration of the helicopter's frame massage my weary soul.

Half an hour out from the firebase, our machines nosed over and the earth floated up to meet us through the mist. Below, everything looked incredibly serene. Little clusters of hooches squatted along the flood plain of a river. There was no movement on the ground, nothing to indicate that anyone was living there. It was as though we were invading a village of ghosts.

A knot formed in my stomach as we neared our target and a feeling of dread crept in. Our final approach always did that to me. We were vulnerable near the ground, perfect targets of fragile machines, blood and bones.

Ed Garcia slammed a magazine into his M-16 and I flinched involuntarily, but my eyes never left the wood line behind the village. I scanned the foliage, looking for little blinks of light, signs that someone was there and they were firing at us. My ears strained to hear the crack of an AK above the roar of our slicks. Then the door gunners opened up and the roar of their M-60's drowned out all other sounds as they hosed down the area. My head exploded and my ears rang. Thick smoke swirled in the slipstream.

The earth was suddenly only three feet away. The slicks hovered and we jumped free, landing in two feet of paddy water. I surged forward looking for a paddy dike to hide behind. I felt naked, totally exposed and I gulped mouthfuls of the humid air. When I finally reached a dike, I fell headlong behind it and lay shoulder deep in the water.

A splash beside me announced the arrival of Garcia. He lay with his head against the dike and looked at me with eyes full of terror. "I hate this, Doc! I hate this!" He exhaled deeply, smirked a little and then added, "I gotta start lookin' for a better job."

The LZ was cold. No return fire. For several minutes we lay panting heavily with our backs against the dike and watched as the choppers disappeared from view. The rain slacked up and became a slow drizzle. Above us, I could hear the steady beat of a gun ship's blades. He circled slowly, invisible in the mist, waiting for our call to unload his ordinance.

"Let's move!" Lt. Gray's shouted order brought us to our feet and we slogged toward the hooches, advancing in four-man fire teams.

In the village, we moved from house to house, searching for weapons or other signs of the enemy. We found none, but then we didn't expect to. The place was inhabited by old men and women, little children and their mothers. The young men were conspicuously absent.

After the search was completed, we settled down inside the hooches to wait for nightfall. We tried to dry our ponchos out and some of the men hung their shirts near the cooking fires. I remember watching Tim Czyzyk remove his boots. He massaged his swollen, wrinkled feet and then pulled a dry pair of socks out of a plastic pouch.

I laughed at him and said, "Czyzyk, what's the deal here? Your boots are soggy. It's still rainin' outside, and the whole world is under water. In a few minutes, you'll be treadin' water in the paddies. So, what's the point?"

He looked at me with a wry grin and said, "Doc, they only issued me two feet when I came into this world. And barring any encounters with a land mine, I'm takin' both of them with me when I leave this place." Then he winked at me and poured the water out of his boots.

It was dusky-dark when we left the village and waded out to our night position. The rain had slowed to the point that it was more like a mist and a pea-soup fog clung to the earth. It was almost impossible to see more than a few feet in front of you, so we walked very close to the man in front of us, following the sounds of his movement. It was bad field discipline. One mine can do a lot of damage under those circumstances. But the fear of getting separated from the others overrode our training. No one wanted to die alone in the dark.

Three hundred yards from the village, the water grew deeper, reaching our thighs. We waded on and the ground beneath us began a gentle slope upward. When the water became only ankle deep, Lt. Gray decided we had found the highest ground we were going to find, so we halted there. There were no dikes around us, so we spread out in a line on the flat, sodden earth to wait.

We hunkered down in the water and stared into the darkness until our eyes hurt. We shivered in the cold. No one attempted to sleep. Instead, we tried to put up a bold front, as though the rain and the darkness and the VC were no match for our bravado, our stamina. We sat like statues, silent sentinels, eternally strong.

A storm rolled through and it started raining hard again. I huddled under my poncho and let my mind go back to the Presidio. I thought about this cute little blonde girl who worked in an adjoining ward to mine. She had always been nice to me when we talked at meals. Sometimes we even walked to work together, since her barracks was not far from mine. Like I said, she was sweet and kind. But here's the weird part. I knew that girl for four months. She smiled at me almost every day. And yet, during all that time, I never once asked her out. Go figure. The more I thought about it, the dumber I got. I mean, here was this sweet, beautiful girl who did everything but beg me for a date and the best I could do was a muttered, "Good morning," from time to time. I was still shaking my head in disbelief when Garcia's whispered question interrupted my thoughts.

"Hey, Doc," he queried, "Is the water getting' deeper, or am I just sinkin' down a little?"

I looked down and realized that Garcia was right. The water was rising.

Then another voice in the darkness. "Hey, Doc! Where are you?" It was Sergeant Boatman, moving toward me.

I grunted to let him know he was near and then he squatted beside me. "Doc, Lt. Gray is thinkin' about movin' again. We need to find some higher ground. He wants you with the CP. Saddle up. Let's go."

When we got to the CP, Gray was huddled under his poncho looking at a map with his red field light. You could see the faint glow coming from the bottom of the shelter, so we sat down to wait. A minute later, the poncho was thrown back and Lt. Gray re-appeared.

"Damn-it!" his muttered oath let me know that the news wasn't good.

"What's the deal?" I asked.

"Well, Doc, it's like this, " Gray spat. "Some idiot at battalion can't read a map. We're right on the assigned coordinates, but were in the middle of a tidal basin. The tide's comin' in and we're trapped. There's nowhere to go. The water behind us is way deep now and there ain't nothin' in front of us but the Mekong River."

"So?" I asked.

"So we're up the proverbial creek. If there's any gooks around and they guess our position, we're like ducks in a barrel.

All we can do is cover up and wait for daylight."

"And pray the water stops rising," offered Sergeant Boatman, "Otherwise, we're swimmin' in the dark."

"Go back to your position, Doc, and pass the word to button up," ordered Gray.

By the time I reached Garcia again, the water was calf-deep.

"What's up?" he asked.

"We're goin' no place, Ed," I began, "Gray says battalion screwed up. We're on an island in the stream. No place to go, amigo, so cover up and hope Chuck (VC) don't find us."

With a sigh of resignation, Garcia disappeared beneath his poncho.

Around midnight, the water stopped rising, cresting nearly knee deep. Another storm passed over and lightning bolts split the sky. I looked back down our line and counted the humps that protruded above the surface. For several hours I sat with my knees drawn up, cradling my aid-bag and using it like a pillow. Occasionally, I dozed off, but I never really slept. Every now and then, I would wipe the mud from my watch face to check the time. I watched the luminous seconds sweep away and I made a little game of trying to guess what time it would be on my next glance. I tried to wish the sun above the horizon.

It was just after three a.m. when I heard the first mortar round. I threw my ponchco back and strained my ears, tracing the path of the deadly missile. At first, there was only a soft whistling sound and then, as it came closer, a high-pitched scream. I opened my mouth to warn the others, but then realized they'd heard it, too. No point.

Seconds passed and the round landed a hundred yards away. There was a funny "whump" when the shell exploded beneath the water and then a gurgle, as if the earth itself had belched. Another round landed slightly closer than the first and that cold, hard knot returned in my gut. More rounds fell, each progressively closer as the enemy gunners walked their explosives in our direction. Next door, I could heat Garcia reciting the Rosary.

Somewhere down the line, I heard a muffled cry, a curse and

then the quick movement of a body through the water. I stared hard into the darkness and in a few seconds Boatman approached moving in a crouch.

"Doc," he asked, "Everybody on this end OK?"

"So far," I answered.

"Well, listen," he explained, "I don't want any noise down here like you just heard up the way. The gooks are firin' blind. They can't see any better'n we can. They're probin', just waitin' for some fool to panic and expose our position. So pass the word. If they aren't hit bad, I don't want any noise. You, Bic?"

I looked at Garcia. He nodded to let me know that he heard the sarge and then he turned to pass the word. I did as ordered – buttoned up and said nothing while the world around me churned in turmoil. The rain came down in sheets and the sound of shrapnel whistling through the air mixed with the rumble of thunder. I don't know how long the barrage lasted. All I can recall is how cold and dark the night was. And how the crashes and the smoke and the gurgling filled my senses. The earth itself seemed to tremble beneath me as I sat with my head between my knees and prayed for it all to end. Occasionally, I would scan around us, trying to spot the flash of their mortar tube, but it was a futile effort. In the heavy rain and fog, you couldn't see fifty yards away.

The worst part of it all was the feeling of helplessness that overwhelmed me. Every now and then, between claps of thunder, I could hear the weird, little "sproink" sound that their tube made as the shell left it. I knew that the VC were very close, but I couldn't see them. And I could hear the round approaching from the sky, but I couldn't see it either. All I could do was curl up and let my imagination run amuck. I kept seeing people heaved into the air in geysers of water and mud with their various body parts sailing away into the night. It made me sick to think that it would be my job to sort out the pieces and parts in the morning. It made me sicker still to think that someone else would be sorting out parts of me.

That's where I was, sorting out parts of me when a mortar

round landed much closer than any of the others. There was a simultaneous splash, explosion and gurgle, followed by an urgent cry of "Medic!"

The cry came only once, but I knew where it came from. I didn't move. I sat blinking back the rain from my eyes. It was like I figured my number was up, too. And if I went down there, down where the wounded man was waiting, I'd be next. I didn't like that idea.

Another clap of thunder, another round straddled us. I threw my poncho off and moved toward the man who needed me.

It was Czyzyk. He was sitting in the water with his arms wrapped around himself, moaning. He smiled weakly when he saw me, then he said, "Doc, I'm damn sure glad to see you. But what took you so long?"

"I didn't hear you at first," I lied. Then the standard question, "Where you hit?"

"My right shoulder," he grimaced and moved his hand. "I don't think it's too bad, but I'm bleedin' like a stuck hog."

I examined his shoulder as best I could under the circumstances, feeling flesh I couldn't really see. There were several small shrapnel holes, but apparently no major damage done. The bleeding had already slowed and Czyzyk could move his shoulder freely.

I handed him my aid-bag and he held it with his good arm while I applied compresses to his wounds. The incoming rounds stopped.

Just as I finished my first aid, Sergeant Boatman arrived on the scene. He sized up the situation for a second, then he smiled and asked, "He gonna make it, Doc?"

"Well, sarge," I returned, "He's got both feet and plenty of blood left. He'll be OK. We can dust him off in the morning. No need to bring in a slick tonight."

Boatman breathed a sigh of relief. "That's what I wanted to hear, Doc. What we don't need right now is anybody exposing us any more than we have to. Can you stay with him, Doc. Maybe keep an eye on him till daybreak?"

"No problem," I answered and Boatman trotted off to check on the other men. The rain slacked up, the tide started to ebb and I gave Czyzyk a shot of morphine. Then I wrapped him in my poncho and sat in weary silence watching him doze, waiting for the sun. In my mind, I kept hearing his innocent query, "What took you so long?"

There didn't seem to be any satisfactory solution for me. I heard his cry. I knew he needed me. And I had a job to do. But I couldn't shake the, "my numbers up" thing. I knew what it was, I just didn't think it would ever happen to me. For some men, the longer they were in the field, the more they felt they were closer to death. It was kind of like, your luck running out, or something like that. But for a medic, such a failure can have fatal results for someone depending on you. And fatal results, for me, would be unforgivable.

When the eastern sky, out toward the South China Sea, began to turn pink, Lt. Gray gave the order to saddle up and we moved back toward the village across the flood plain. Garcia and Coniglio helped me with Czyzyk and even then it was difficult. The ground we crossed was nothing more than knee-deep mud that sucked your energy out in no time. It was well after sunup when we reached the high ground.

While we waited for the dust-off, I sat with Czyzyk, making small talk with him. I remember how grateful he was and how he kept saying what a great medic I was. He only added more guilt to my conscience and I tried to steer the conversation to other topics. Like his trip to Japan, or possibly stateside. But he ignored my remarks, and told again how the explosions just kept roaring and how scared he was when the shrapnel hit him.

"I thought I was gonna die, Doc. All I could think about was how much it hurt and how my blood kept oozing between my fingers. You'll never know how glad I was to see your face last night, Doc. I'll never forget you for what you've done," he promised.

It was later in the morning, after Czyzyk had been dusted off, that I finally got some help sorting out what had occurred. I was sitting alone, smoking a cigarette and gazing out at the river. Someone sat down beside me and I looked over to see Sergeant Boatman.

I cleared my throat and started to speak. An apology in the offing. But before my words were formed, Boatman offered some of his own.

"You know, Doc," he began, "Tides are kind of interesting. In a way, they're really hard to figure out. I mean, they come in, they go out. They ebb and they flow. It's hard to believe that the moon and the earth's spin have anything to do with it. A real scientific mystery, ya know?"

"Yeah, I guess you're right sarge," I answered.

"Ya know something, Doc?" Boatman offered, "men are a lot like tides. Sometimes one way, sometimes another. And our courage is like a tide, it ebbs and flows. Men are often brave and sometimes cowards, but the truth is, we're all somewhere in between. You just gotta go with the flow."

Fear

Going anywhere in Vietnam was inherently dangerous - to the latrine, or just taking out the garbage. I once knew a cook who lifted the lid on a garbage can and found a hand frag under it. He's dead now. Nothing was sacred, nothing was safe and you could never be sure of anything.

To protect our sanity, we pretended that we weren't there at all and our vocabulary reflected that posture. We were in the Nam, a violent, unforgiving place that existed somewhere outside the boundaries of the universe. Our friends and relatives were back in the world. And there was absolutely no connection between those two realms.

No one died in Vietnam. At least we didn't say the word "died," or "dead." We used terms like "wasted," or "zapped." And we didn't kill our enemies, either. We "brought smoke on them," which was perfectly all right since they weren't real people. They were only gooks named "Chuck," or "Charlie."

Fear was our constant companion. To be sure, we feared dying, but beyond that and greater still was the fear that we might fail our friends in a time of need. We didn't vocalize our fears very often, and if we did, we only joked about them. Making things humorous gave our situation a cartoon-like, surreal quality. It made things less painful, softened reality.

Only one man ever confessed his fear to me in a serious vein and the courage he exhibited in doing so still inspires me. His name was Ed Garcia. He was a twenty-year-old buck sergeant, my squad leader and my friend. His confession came at the end of a long day in the field. We were sitting in the shade of a hooch, just eating some C's before a night op. Ed suddenly sat his can of peaches down and he gave me this look. It made me uncomfortable. Really.

He just sat the can down and he gave me this look and I knew something serious was coming. "I'm losin' it, Doc," he murmured. "I don't know how much longer I can do this. Ya know?"

Like all men, anytime something really gut-wrenching comes up, I played dumb. "What-a-ya mean?" I mused, staring at my turkey loaf.

"I mean… well…. damn-it, Doc. Every time we come into an LZ now… and those guns start goin' off…" His voiced dropped as though he were telling me his deepest, darkest secret, "I'm terrified, Doc. When all that stuff starts happening…. Well… I'm just terrified, that's all."

I looked into his eyes before I answered. I really did. And I saw exactly what he was trying to tell me. I saw a fear that went beyond any fear I had known and yet, he had this steely, determined look, too. I can't describe it exactly. I mean, if you've ever seen it – you'd know it. Otherwise…. well it was weird, that's all.

So anyway, I looked right back at him and I'll never forget what happened next. He didn't wait for my answer. For true. He just got up and walked away. Left me sitting with a spoon dangling from my fingers. It was like he already knew what he had to do and because we loved like brothers, he would do what was necessary rather than fail a friend. And he did, until the day he died.

We were sweeping a line of nipa palms in the delta west of Ben Luc. The monsoon rains had fallen all day and turned the trail we were following into a thick, boot-sucking mire that drained you a little at a time. Moving one foot in front of the other became an exhausting chore. Our rain-soaked uniforms hung heavily from our bodies and pulled us deeper into the earth. We were chilled to the bone. In the rain and mist, visibility was a hopeless dream. No one saw the bunker sitting in the thick undergrowth near the trail.

Ramos, the point man, moved slowly past it and three steps behind came Bob Cole. As Garcia drew even with the bunker, he hesitated for an instant, like maybe he heard something. Then, just as he started to move again, a prolonged, staccato explosion split the air and reverberated off the walls of the jungle. The rest of our squad lunged forward and lay with our faces pressed into the mud. The whole world seemed to erupt in explosions as the rear element of the third platoon opened fire on the bunker. In a matter of seconds, it was totally destroyed along with a large patch of the jungle.

The echoes of the gunfire died away, replaced by a peculiar quiet. The only sounds were those of the rain spattering on the trail and dripping from the surrounding foliage. The smoke from our weapons lay thick in the humid air and clung to the earth, refusing to rise. I remember how strange it was to look up that trail and see nothing but smoke mixed with the heavy mist. And how the air tasted. It had this awful acid-like taste and odor from the gunpowder. I remember the scream that brought me to my feet and pulled me into the ghostly veil where I found Ed and the others.

I was only twenty feet behind them and yet it was difficult to see where they had fallen. I was almost on top of them before I spotted the bodies. Just a quick check of each man was all I needed. There was no chance I would miss-diagnose these casualties. Each man had caught a full burst from the AK in his upper body. No chance. They had absolutely no chance and probably never had time to react.

I set some men to work bagging up Ramos and Cole in their ponchos, but I saved Ed for myself. He was my amigo. He deserved better than he got and I didn't want anyone else to handle that final chore. I remember kneeling over his lifeless body sprawled in the mud. His jungle hat had flown off somewhere and his dark hair had fallen into his face. Fresh blood oozed from his wounds. It mixed with the raindrops and ran in little rivulets off his body, forming rivers of bright red on the surface of the trail.

I smoothed his hair back and I remember looking into his dark, Latin eyes. And I thought about what I had seen there the last time I looked. I thought about his confession and I thought about what he had sacrificed rather than give in to fear. Then I closed his eyes gently for him, wrapped him in his poncho and we moved back down the trail into the mist.

Sometimes, in my dreams, I still see Ed. But he's not lying in the mud. He's sitting in the door of a helicopter as we charge through the sky above the lush, delta landscape. His hat is off and his hair is blowing in the slipstream. He lifts his hand and waves to me in an adjoining ship. He's grinning, like a kid on a carnival ride and in his face, I see no fear.

Taps

The flag was at half-staff hanging limp and lifeless in a slate gray sky. There was no breeze to stir the colors and even though it was very early in the day, the air was already pregnant with the moisture of the monsoons. Tiny beads of sweat formed on my forehead as I stood alone in the street outside battalion headquarters. Beneath the flagpole stood a large, white concrete monument painted with our unit crest and the motto, "To The Utmost Extent Of Our Power." For Ramos, Cole and Ed Garcia, the words proved to be their epitaph.

In front of the monument stood the objects which had drawn me to that place. Three M-16's with bayonets affixed had been pushed into the soft earth. On the butt of each rifle sat a helmet, their camouflaged covers wet with the night's rainfall. A bright green kerchief was tied around the front of each helmet, forming a mask where the man's face should have been. And embroidered on each kerchief were the words, "Bravo Company- Cong Killers Hardcore." A set of empty boots rested on the ground in front of each weapon.

As I stood surveying the scene, my eyes moved slowly from one memorial to the next. At each stop, I envisioned the faces of the men who were now gone.

Ramos came to mind first. I suppose because he was usually walking point when we made our sweeps. I smiled slightly as I recalled the way he carried himself. He never exhibited fear, though I was sure he had felt it. Ramos seemed totally at ease, not careless, but relaxed and confident. He laughed often and always had a new joke to tell, bringing humor when it was sorely needed.

Bob Cole filled the second set of boots. I couldn't help but brush my mustache softly as I thought of him. Bob was a full-blooded Cherokee, practically devoid of facial hair. His one ambition in life had been to grow a mustache so prolific that he would be court-martialed for failure to comply with proper military standards. When we were in the field, Bob would caution me to sleep lightly or he would scalp my upper lip - claiming for himself something God and genetics had denied him.

The last set of boots belonged to my friend, Ed Garcia. To my mind, he was the bravest of them all. When my eyes rested on his mask, he spoke to me again his haunting confession of terror. It kindled in me afresh an overpowering sense of admiration and brought to me the true meaning of heroism. In the midst of his fear, Garcia found the courage to overpower it and soldier on. He humped the paddies carrying a terrible load. But he never laid it down and he never quit. In the end, it finally pulled him into the rich soil of the delta.

Standing there, on that spot of earth, I came to appreciate the simple truth of what I saw. It was a fitting memorial, bearing mute testimony to the way they lived. They soldiered with their feet and legs, with all the muscle, bone and blood they possessed. And ultimately, to the utmost extent.

When my personal memorial service was over, I walked to the chapel to attend an official one. The chaplain did the best he could. He spoke briefly about duty, honor and country. Then he added a few thoughts about the briefness of life and the certainty of eternal rewards.

It was the end of the service that remains with me, even today. As we stood saluting the colors, a bugler played a final tribute. It was the song of my soul that echoed in the tranquil air that morning and I can still hear myself whispering softly the words to "Taps."

The Phone

At some point in time during my tour, I called home. I don't remember exactly when it was. I only remember that it was very hot and wet. We were on a three-day stand-down and during our break we were allowed to put our name on a waiting list to use the newly installed MARS setup.

MARS was a radio hook-up which jumped from one HAM radio station to another and was somehow connected to the telephone system in the continental United States. In one sense, it was a technological triumph and an incredible gift to us. We could actually make a phone call and talk to our loved ones as though we were just across town.

On the other hand, it was almost too weird for words. I mean, you're sitting in the Mekong Delta, helicopters are coming and going and an artillery battery is firing huge chunks of death into the air. Meanwhile, you're on the phone with your mother telling her everything is just fine. Don't worry. Yeah, right.

My turn came to make the call on the third day. I had to squeeze the conversation in around my preparation to go back to the bush that night. It made the call all that more difficult. I mean, the thought did cross my mind that I could get off the phone with my mother and within an hour or two get wasted. Technology is a wondrous gift.

I remember sitting in the Commo (communications) shed and watching the other men come out of the booth, some with red eyes and others smiling. I kept thinking that maybe the call wasn't such a good idea and at one point, I almost told the radio tech to forget it. But then I found myself inside the booth and the call was made.

I don't remember whether or not I actually heard the phone ring in my parents' house. I think someone else spoke to her first, explaining how the net operated and instructing her to say "over," each time she finished her end of the conversation. I do remember how pensive I was and how bewildered my mother's voice sounded when she first spoke to me.

"Hello, mom! Over," I almost shouted.

"Hel... Hello? Is that you, son?" she asked.

Somewhere in the world, a bemused HAM operator said, "Say over, ma'am."

"You mean me?" mom asked.

"Yes, ma'am. I need to know when you're finished so I can transmit. OK?"

"Oh...Oh, I see. Well... Over!" mom stammered.

"Yes," I laughed. "This is your son! Over."

"I can't believe this," mom's voiced cracked with emotion. "Where are you, son? Are you alright?"

Again, the radio operator, "Say over, ma'am."

"Oh yes. Over!" mom croaked.

"Yes, mom, I'm just fine. I'm not hurt. I'm just taking advantage of a new radio hook-up to give you a call. This is gonna be kind of brief, we're very limited on time. Lot of other guys wanna use the phone. Over." I joked.

"Well, I wish your father was here," mom exclaimed. "He sure would like to hear your voice. You know we worry about you, son. Are you in any danger?"

"Please say, over, ma'am," the radioman pleaded.

"Oh, I'm sorry, dear. I'm just not used to this kind of call. I'll do better. I promise," mom answered.

"Thank you, ma'am. Just say, over. OK?" came his terse reply.

"Over!" mom muttered emphatically.

"No, mom," I lied. "I'm not in any danger. Everything here is very safe. Where's dad off to? Over." I asked.

"He's up in eastern Kentucky with the pipeline. I reckon he'll be home this weekend. Are you sure everything is alright? You're not hurt or anything are you? Over."

"No, mom, I'm not hurt. I'm at our base camp. Have you seen Debbie lately? Over."

"Yes, son. She was here just the other day. She brought some of your letters over for me to read. It sounds like a dangerous place, son. I'm praying for you. Over."

The commo man signaled that I was going to have to cut my conversation off soon, so I tried to wind up my visit home.

"Mom, I'm going to have to get off the net soon. Just tell everyone that I send my love and tell them that I'm OK. Over."

"Alright, son," she sniffed. "I'll tell the family how you're doing. But are you eating good? In the pictures you've sent, you look like skin and bones. Don't they feed you a proper meal? Over."

I shrugged at the radio operator.

"Yes, mom, they feed us just fine. It's just with the heat and all, I guess my appetite is a little depressed. When I get home, you can fatten me up. OK? Over."

"Well, son, I know you'll be alright. I've asked the Lord to look after you. But still, I worry sometimes. That place over there looks just awful on television. I've got to where I won't watch the TV news anymore. You're not in any of that shooting are you? Over."

"Of course not," I lied again. "I'm in Rach Kien most of the time. I've got to go now, mom. Their signaling me to let someone else have the phone. Over"

There was a brief pause and I could tell that my mother was trying to get control of her emotions. Then, with her voice cracking, she finished her conversation.

"Alright, son. I understand. I'm glad you got to call. It's so good to hear your voice. I pray you'll be home soon, safe and sound. I love you, son."

My face flushed. My voice was choked. A thousand thoughts raced across my brain. Deep within me, a voice cried out, urging me to release the pain. But I couldn't. It wasn't hers to bear. I couldn't tell her about Charlie Sheppard and how I couldn't save him. There was no power within my soul to confess my fear and how it felt to put Ed Garcia in his cocoon. Words were inadequate to convey the feelings of the heart.

So I clutched the receiver gingerly to my face and whispered, "Goodbye, mother. I love you," into the now dead phone.

Magic

During stand-downs, we were often sent out on patrols near the firebase. There was seldom any enemy activity nearby and to most of us, the local operations were considered nothing more than a nuisance. A little device used by battalion to deny us a decent night's sleep and keep us busy. Each evening, four teams made up from inactive platoons, were sent north, south, east and west of Rach Kien to serve as LP's for the firebase.

We called these operations, local bushes. And two weeks before I left the line, we were the one's who got local bushed.

We were south of the firebase and things had been so quiet there, we should have known we were due for something to pop. But inactivity can lull you into a sense of security, like maybe the VC had left, or run out of ammunition.

At four o'clock, we left the firebase and walked through the ville. The heat was intense and the mosquitoes out early. I could hear other men slapping at them as we moved along, with our boots sinking into the muddy road. It would be another damp night.

When we reached the proper grid coordinates, we turned west and walked toward the setting sun. I remember the horizon that evening was a virtual explosion of color and the nipa palms stood outlined in shades of purple and orange. I remarked to Joe McCarthy, who was walking behind me, that the sunset was a feast for the eyes. But Joe had his own perspective and remarked, "Sun goes down. Gooks come out. Don't like it, Doc. They can paint it any color they want, but I still hate it." So much for the beauty of nature.

Half a click from the road, we spread out along some dikes and waited for darkness. Most of us took the opportunity to smoke our last cigarette and splash bug juice on our bodies. Spider Dixon performed his ritual radio check to make sure battalion had us on the correct frequency. Darkness closed in and no one spoke. It was so quiet, you could hear a mosquito coming fifty yards away.

They hit us just as we started to stand up for our final move. The wood line before us lit up like a Christmas tree and the chilling sound of exploding rifles cracked like a popcorn popper. If they had waited just a split second longer, the VC would have run up a pretty good body count. But they weren't patient enough, or an angel was on hand. I was still half bent over when the first rounds zipped by so close I could feel the wind off them.

remember collapsing to the earth instantly, but it felt like the ground was miles away. I was sure death had finally caught up with me. Up and down the line, I could hear muffled curses as the rest of the platoon hunkered down and began to return fire. The night became a steady roar of explosions.

Someone touched my elbow and I turned to see Sergeant Boatman grinning at me. "You hit, Doc?" he asked. I just shook my head to let him know I was OK and he began to move on down the line. Then he turned and half-shouted to me, "Doc, since you ain't firin' nothin', watch our rear. I don't want them gooks outflankin' us!" I nodded to let him know that I heard him and flipped over to peer into the gloom.

There was no movement, other than enemy tracer rounds, which bounced and floated toward the horizon. I was lying with my chin on my aid-bag when our artillery started screaming in and the enemy firing ceased. The barrage lasted about five minutes and then we were up on line, walking through the swirling smoke and orange shadows.

The jungle was silent and empty and void of any evidence that anyone had been there. It was as though we had been bushed by phantoms, who disappeared into the twisted, burning wreckage of the night.

We searched for half an hour trying to re-establish contact with the VC, but much to our relief, they chose not to be found. So we moved back out into the paddies and set up in a new location, hoping to get a little sleep. It was a vain hope - sleep was denied. We got a nightmare instead.

Our terror came in the form of artillery rounds, which suddenly began landing all around us. I remember lifting my head and turning my ear toward the sound when the first shell screamed overhead. It didn't make sense. Why were they firing again? And why were they walking the shells in our direction? They were landing so close, that the force of their explosions lifted us off the ground.

Lt. Gray grabbed the radio and raised battalion while the rest of us curled ourselves into the fetal position. The smaller the target, the better. Above the ear-splitting roars, I could hear Gray arguing with headquarters.

"Don't tell me these shells can't be close to us!" he yelled into the phone. "I'm laying in a damn crater! Now shut it off!"

Just as Lt. Gray slammed the receiver down, I heard the last shell arcing in on us. I could tell from the sound that this one was right on target and I lay paralyzed with fear, waiting for its arrival. The sound of the approaching shell grew louder until it filled my ears. The world stopped. Disjointed thoughts. Then a tremendous rush of wind moved over me and I remember an instantaneous thought that the rush would be the last sound I would ever hear. But it wasn't.

There was this loud, "smack!" and the shell pancaked into the mud only a few feet from where I lay. Then a hissing sound as the hot metal scorched the water around it. I lay quite still for a second or two before I realized that I was actually still alive. Then I sat up and looked over at where the shell lay, steaming in the mud. I blinked my eyes to make sure of what I saw and I started to say something, but no words came out. My mouth felt like cotton. My tongue was stuck in my dry throat.

I was still sitting that way, shaking in disbelief when Sergeant Boatman walked over and patted me on the head. "You lead a charmed life, Doc. I ain't never seen anything like it."

I just grinned at him and collapsed against the paddy dike, too weak to answer.

Then he squatted down, rubbed my head and whispered softly, "Let me get a little more of that magic."

Hearts

The first week of June, I made my last trip out to Gook Village. It was early morning when the Mad Dogs dropped us off in the sleepy hamlet. Only a few dogs and old people were stirring. For our part, there was very little movement involved. We weren't there to search the village, or shake down the local populace. We were there to hook up with an ARVN unit. They were supposed to bring a prisoner with them who could reveal the location of a large weapons cache which intelligence said was nearby. It was a long wait. The ARVN's were late as usual.

A rain squall sprang up while we waited, so we huddled under our ponchos as we sat on a paddy dike and tried to smoke soggy cigarettes. Somewhere in the village, a small child was crying.

"Doc," Joe McCarthy asked mournfully, "Why 'zit always rainin' when we make these sweeps? Why can't we get at least enough dry time to play a hand or two of Hearts while we wait?"

I started to answer, but he didn't give me time before he started again. "And besides, how come we always hookin' up with these gook outfits? Seems like we're forever messin' around with Marvin the Arvin. I don't like this, Doc. Don't trust 'em."

"At least we're not out in the reeds," I offered. "I'm too close to home for that."

Joe smiled at my comment. He thought about it for a minute, then he offered a little sage advise. "Doc, we go out there before the new doc arrives, you best pull a sham of some kind. You know, belly ache, the trots, somethin'. You don't even wanna make another run out there. That place is number ten."

"You know it," I replied as I snuffed out my smoke and closed my eyes.

Around ten o'clock, the rain stopped and the ARVN's dropped in. Their commander was a skinny little lieutenant, who wore a gold Seiko wristwatch the size of a wall clock.

Their prisoner turned out to be a young woman. She may have been considered pretty at one time in her life, but not that day. Her hair was matted with mud. Her face was swollen and she glanced around furtively like a captured beast. Her hands were tied behind her with parachute cords that cut deeply at the wrists and she was being pulled along roughly by a heavy rope, which was tied around her fragile neck. The black silk clothing she wore was torn in numerous places exposing her nakedness and bruises.

All in all she was a pitiful sight, but she wasn't under our control, so after a brief introduction, Lt. Gray ordered us to fall in behind the ARVN unit. We followed them across the flooded paddies with the woman leading the way.

"Look at it this way, Doc," chuckled McCarthy, "We got ourselves a first-class mine detector."

An hour later, we reached some dry ground, so the ARVN's decided it was time for a lunch break. We ate C's, the ARVN's had dog meat and rice. The woman had nothing. She squatted alone in the center of our formation, blindfolded during the break. I guess the ARVN lieutenant didn't want her to steal any culinary secrets.

As we ate, I couldn't help watching the prisoner. And I couldn't help feeling ashamed of the way she was being treated. To me, it wasn't about which side was right. It wasn't about what she may have done. It was about who would show mercy, who would show kindness. Who would be truly human.

I sat for a long time thinking about that. And then I opened a can of pears and moved toward the woman. Coniglio saw what I was up to and grabbed my arm. "Doc," he muttered under his breath, "I wouldn't do that if I were you. Marvin the Arvin ain't gonna like it."

"Screw Marvin," I spat, as I broke his grip.

When I reached the woman, I squatted down and spoke to her quietly, "Me Bouxi. Number one chop, chop." Then I opened my canteen and lifted it to her lips. Everything got really quiet. I heard footsteps behind me, but I ignored them and placed the can of fruit in her hands. An angry shout burst in my ears and a quick kick sent the pears sailing away. The woman hunched down and covered her head while I whirled to face the intruder. It was the ARVN lieutenant and he was totally bent out of shape.

He screamed at me in a high-pitched voice filled with rage. I glared back at him and felt the back of my neck getting hotter by the second. I was within a heartbeat of taking a swing at Johnny Wallclock when Lt. Gray stepped in between us.

"Back off, Doc!" he yelled.

I didn't move. My feet were frozen to the ground.

Gray got right in my face and muttered fiercely, "Doc, you're outta line! I said, get away from here!"

I squatted back down and whispered to the woman, then I moved slowly back to join the other men while Gray conferred with the ARVN commander. After a few minutes, they shook hands and Gray came over to where I was sitting.

"Look, Doc," he began, "Like it or not, this is not our show. Now I've smoothed things over, so stay cool. These people don't go for philanthropy."

We spent another half hour wading in the paddies and then we split up. The first squad went into a wood line with the ARVN's, supposedly to retrieve the weapons cache. The second squad, with me included, was assigned area security. We set up in a local burial ground, resting against the tombstones.

Ten minutes into our wait, McCarthy and Coniglio came over to my position. They wanted to play a game of Hearts to pass the time. It was poor field discipline, but we played anyway.

I guess it was after our third, or fourth hand, that the first squad re-emerged from the undergrowth. They weren't carrying anything except what they went into the woods with. Then the ARVN unit came out and they were empty handed, too. I remember pointedly that I looked for my nemesis, the ARVN lieutenant. I figured he'd be upset about finding nothing and I wanted to see the look on his face. But he was missing from their formation. So was the woman.

McCarthy broke my train of thought. "Hey, Doc. Deal the

cards, man. We'll be leavin' in a few minutes."

I nodded and I looked again at the moving line of men.

"Doc, you gonna..." McCarthy started.

But his words were shattered by the sound of a single shot that rang out from the tree line.

Instinctively, I grabbed my aid-bag and started to get up. But McCarthy grabbed my arm and pulled me back down.

"Doc," he said angrily, "Nobody's callin' for a medic, and besides, it's your turn to deal. We got to play Hearts."

Hands

He was the bravest man I ever knew. Real Congressional Medal of Honor material. Did his job with total abandon and no regard for personal safety. He felt that his position as a medic was nothing less than a sacred trust and that the lives of his men, the guys in his platoon, were given into his care by God himself. He shouldered that responsibility without regret and I never heard him complain about it. His name was Jon Robertson. He's dead now, but his name lives forever in the polished, black surface of a memorial.

Jon had one love in his life beyond his job and that was Hue, our Vietnamese interpreter. Hue was a well educated young woman of striking beauty and she came from an influential family in the village of Rach Kien. Jon and Hue had a romance going. I don't mean a physical thing, even though the desire was there. It was this emotional, maybe even a spiritual thing. You could see it in their eyes any time they were near each other.

The romance could have gone all the way to the altar as far as Jon was concerned, but Hue's parents didn't like the idea at all. They forbade Hue to see Jon, fearing he would convince her to leave Vietnam. They didn't want her to end up in America, where she might be viewed as just another Asian gold-digger.

Losing Hue was a hard blow for Jon to bear and in May, when a new recon company was formed, he volunteered to serve as their medic. The new platoon spent most of their time in the bush, working in the roughest areas. That suited Jon just fine. He didn't care where he was, as long as he didn't have to watch Hue come and go every day.

The Recon Company was commanded by 1st Lieutenant James Lawson. He had been a platoon leader in Bravo Company, but when he heard about recon, he jumped at the chance to command his own outfit. Lt. Lawson wasn't power hungry, he just had his own ideas about how to conduct a guerilla war and he was often at odds with the hierarchy at battalion. I guess you could say he was a maverick of sorts and he quickly gathered a large following of like-minded men.

The Recon Company quickly became the hotspot of the 5th/60th. They were always in the thick of any fighting and they loved it. On the breast pocket of their camouflaged fatigues, they wore a patch that proclaimed ominously, "No Quarter Asked - None Given."

In the third week of June, the third herd pulled duty in conjunction with the Recon Company. My replacement had arrived and I knew that a job at the aid-station was very close to a reality for me. The last place in the world I wanted to be, was anywhere Recon had chosen. Their presence could only mean one thing - a shooting war. And I'd had all of that I wanted. But Lt. Gray asked me to stay around for a few days to help the new medic get his feet on the ground and that left me with no choice but to go along on one last eagle flight.

We caught our lift-out early in the morning, just as heavy, dark clouds were building on the horizon. The air was hot and still. As we flew toward the LZ, I sat in the door of the slick looking at the lush earth. With the advent of the rains, the countryside had greened out and everything looked renewed. The paddies were flooded and full of ripening rice, the canals and rivers were overflowing and the nipa palms even took on a deeper hue. I remember losing myself in the greenness of it all and thinking how much I would miss that part of the war. I was like a god, moving above my pregnant domain, brooding over the ripening fruit, waiting for a birthing. It was the Garden of Eden, with an evil twist.

Joe McCarthy was sitting beside me in the doorway, cradling his M-60 in his lap. He leaned over to me and shouted, "Doc, if we didn't have to go down there and hump them paddies, this place would be beautiful, man. I mean, from up here it is!"

He paused a second and then asked, " Didn't Sherman say, "War is hell"?" I nodded.

"Well, he was only part right," Joe offered.

"How so?" I yelled back.

"It's hell warmed over!" he returned with a wink.

A few minutes later, our target came into view. A small cluster of hooches nestled among the fields of green. As we flew over the village, I noticed that there was no movement on the ground. The place looked deserted, and that was an ill omen. It was as though they knew we were coming and a reception had been arranged.

On the west side of the villsage, a small river snaked across the land and we were dropped on the far side of it. There was no firing from the door gunners, no prepping from a gunship. Nothing. Just pure serenity defiled by our chopper blades. When we were three feet off the ground, the slicks hovered and we jumped free to land in Eden.

I watched the slicks wheel away and wished desperately that I was on one of them. Then I joined the rest of the platoon as we spread out along the banks of the river to form a blocking unit and we waited for the arrival of the Recon Company.

The clouds that had been brewing moisture opened up and a steady rain began to fall. Across the canal, through sheets of rain and mist, the village lay silent before us. Funny as it sounds, we spoke to each other in hoarse whispers as though we had arrived cloaked in secrecy and the people huddled in their hooches didn't know we were hiding behind the curtain of rain.

A few minutes later, the sound of blades biting into the sky announced the arrival of Recon. Their lift dropped them on the far side of the village and sailed away. Above us in the clouds, I could hear a gunship orbiting unseen, waiting for the action to begin.

As I peered through the downpour, I could see the Recon Company begin their sweep, sprinting across the paddies in four-man fire teams. They looked like ghosts, floating in the mist.

When the final fire team entered the village, they began moving house to house. Sporadic firing and explosions broke out as Recon moved among the hooches, spraying them with small arms fire and tossing hand frags through the doors. As best I could tell, there was no return fire. At least, not in the beginning.

There was nothing for us to do except to lay low and watch the violence unfold like kids watching a 3-D movie. The new medic lay beside me, breathing hard and looking at me with fear in his eyes. I knew how he felt. I knew what he was thinking. And I knew that he would have to decide for himself when the time came, how he was going to deal with the craziness and the insane, senseless, deadly game called war.

The situation came to a head when the Recon Company reached the near side of the village, just across the river from us. They were only a hundred yards away at that point and I could see them clearly in spite of the downpour. The number one fire team was squatting against the wall of a hooch and the second fire team, with Lt. Lawson, was just moving around them, running in a crouch, when the heavy thud of a Chicom machine gun split the air.

I watched in horror as four men crumpled instantly. Three of them fell straight down as if an invisible hand had swept them from the earth. But the fourth man, Lt. Lawson, staggered sideways and fell into an open cistern. I could only watch helplessly as his hand came out of the water and he tried desperately to grasp the edge of the deep well. But the earth was soggy and the edges of the cistern were nothing but slick mud. He couldn't get a handhold.

Amid the noise and confusion of all the firing, it was difficult to sort out exactly what was happening. Men were running, shooting and shouting. Our platoon had opened up on full bore and the world became a roar of explosions. Then, out of the mist, I saw a solitary figure rush toward the cistern. It was Jon.

He sprinted flat out, not bothering to duck or weave and he almost made it. But just as he neared Lt. Lawson, he came under direct fire from the Chicom and he, too, wilted under its deadly spray. Jon fell headlong, arms extended and he died almost touching Lawson's hands.

The Wallet

We were on the outskirts of Saigon, snarled in traffic and barely moving when a young girl jumped up on the running board of the battalion water truck. She looked about twelve years old, but she knew the ropes.

"You, you, you," she laughed out to us. "You number one GI. You want cold coke?" she asked demurely. "Traffic number ten today. You no go anywhere. You stop? Cold coke?" she continued.

Wayne Hawkins, who was driving looked at his co-driver and I. "Either of you in a hurry?" he asked.

"Not me," his sidekick answered.

"Just so I get to Third Field Hospital before noon," I added.

"Well, in that case, I guess we'll pull over for a few minutes and let this traffic clear out a little," Wayne said.

The coke-girl giggled loudly when Wayne pulled off the road. She sprang free as soon as we stopped and ran to get us our drinks, which were as promised - icy cold.

We took refuge from the sun in the shade of the truck, sipping our drinks and rinsing the dust from our throats. I closed my eyes and listened to the soft, sticky hum of tires on passing vehicles as they rolled slowly through the melted tar of Highway 4. Every now and then, a heat wave, pungent with diesel fumes, rippled past.

The girl didn't leave while we drank. Instead, she stood beside the assistant driver and gently stroked his hair. When the drinks were finished, the girl collected the bottles and then she hit us with a new proposition.

"You want boom, boom?" she asked. "Sister is number one girl. Very good. You pay five dow for number one boom, boom?"

Wayne and I both gave a negative answer, but the co-driver offered only a slight snicker.

The girl decided to try a more effective sales promotion. She lifted her blouse to expose herself. "Me te-te," she said. "But sister is beaucoup, very nice. Number one!"

The co-driver smiled broadly at the girl's antics. He reached out to touch her.

Wayne stood up, cleared his throat and stood staring across the adjacent paddies. I was stunned by what was happening and didn't know what to do. A sense of shame came over me and I walked around to the back of the truck. For a moment or two, I stood looking down the highway at the coke stands that dotted the right-of-way, and a sense of anger began to rise in me. I saw the price that desperation extracts from a people. I saw them selling anything they could lay their hands on, and when there was nothing else left to market, they put their children on the auction block.

I became incensed about the whole situation, as though the entire problem of little girls and sex for sale was mine to deal with. So I started back for the front of the truck to confront Wayne's helper. But my confrontation never happened. Wayne beat me to the punch.

I rounded the front fender of the truck just in time to see Wayne land a vicious right hook on his buddy's jaw. There was a loud "pop," the man's eyes rolled back in his head and he crumpled to the pavement with Wayne astride him.

I thought a beating was about to occur, so I lunged forward to restrain Wayne. But he pushed me away and shouted, "I ain't gonna hit him again, Doc. He wouldn't feel it anyway."

Then he started going through the man's pockets and chuckled out loud when he withdrew a large wad of MPC's. He tossed the crumpled bills to the little girl and as she was eagerly scooping them up, Wayne said with a wry grin, "If ya' really wanna' hurt a man, Doc, ya gotta hit him in the wallet."

Schroder

He was old and ugly, a mixed breed with no pure bloodline and he moved about the firebase on short, crooked legs, waddling like a drunk. His floppy ears were notched and his compact body scarred in numerous places. No one claimed ownership where he was concerned and so he belonged to everyone. Schroder was our unofficial mascot. A free spirit who roamed at will among us begging food and sleeping wherever he pleased. As dogs go, he wasn't much, but Schroder was all we had and everyone loved him. Everyone that is, except the colonel, who looked upon him as nothing more than a nuisance and a constant source of trouble.

The colonel's dislike for Schroder didn't seem to bother the dog much. He took the colonel's kicks and curses with hardened indifference. Like the rest of us, he considered our commander just another one of life's inconveniences that had to be put up with, so Schroder didn't let the colonel cramp his style. He and our commander played an on-going, un-ending game of one upmanship, each one waiting to see what the other would do next.

Schroder relished the competition. Of all the places on the firebase he could choose for his afternoon nap, it was usually battalion headquarters that was graced with his presence. It was as though he lay there in ambush, just waiting for an opportunity to challenge his enemy.

The battle of wits came to a head when our division commander came to visit. It was supposed to be a surprise visit, but the colonel's intelligence net was performing admirably and we had plenty of advance warning. We spent the entire week before the general arrived polishing everything in sight.

The mess hall got a new coat of paint and all troops were under strict orders to wear only clean uniforms and polished boots if they appeared outside the barracks during the general's stopover. It was a big occasion for the colonel and he wanted to make sure his unit represented him well. Everyone did, except Shroder.

On the morning of the general's visit, Schroder came strutting down the main street of the firebase wearing sunglasses and a bright, yellow tee shirt decorated with a South Vietnamese flag and the words "Chu-hoi" painted on it.

The shirts were the clever invention of someone at MAC-V in Saigon. They were supposed to be given away to the children in our area, along with leaflets, which encouraged the VC to "Chu-hoi," or give up and join our side. I don't know how Schroder ended up with one of those tee shirts, but it fit him exceptionally well.

Schroder and the general's entourage arrived at battalion headquarters at precisely the same moment. It was a perfectly timed operation. As the general stepped from his jeep to return our battalion commander's salute, Schroder executed a salute of his own. His left, rear leg snapped to a ninety degree angle and he deftly sprayed the rear tire of the general's spotless machine.

Under the circumstances, there was nothing the colonel could do, except to quickly hustle the general indoors before he became aware of the incident. With his mission completed, Schroder, basking in the glow of victory, ambled off to the mess hall for his mid-morning snack.

Two hours and several hot dogs later, Schroder returned to the headquarters building for his mid-day siesta. He was dozing quietly near the front door with an unfinished tubesteak near his nose when the colonel's briefing ended and the brass began filing out.

As he stepped out the front door, the colonel spied Schroder and general or no, he was determined to get even with the dog. He made a little sidestep and attempted a quick, soccer-style kick at his favorite target. But as he did so, he made the mistake of planting his left foot on Schroder's unfinished meal. The results of his error were disastrous.

The colonel went airborne - arms flailing, feet reaching for terra firma. Major Hanson, who was walking behind him, tried to catch the colonel, but it was a futile effort. They both ended up flat on their backs. The general heard the commotion and turned round just in time to catch a glimpse of Schroder as he made his escape. His jaw dropped. He shook his head. His staff helped the colonel and Major Hanson to their feet.

The general waited a moment to let the colonel recover his dignity. Then he pursed his lips and asked, "Was that a dog in a tee shirt I saw just now?"

The colonel, caught off-guard and still stinging with humiliation, gave the general this blank, dumbfounded stare. "What dog?" he asked.

"The one with sunglasses on," the general stated flatly.

"Sunglasses? I'm sure there's nothing like that around here, sir!" came the reply.

"Well.... Carry on!" snapped the general as he got in his jeep.

The colonel waited until the general's convoy was out of sight and then he went for his pistol.

Meanwhile, Schroder had ambled out to the front gate to mooch candy from the gate guard. He was sitting beside the guard shack when the general pulled up. The guard tried to screen Schroder, but the general saw him and within seconds it was over.

An adjutant jumped out and scooped up Schroder. The convoy started moving again and the last any of us saw of Schroder, his pudgy, sunglassed face was gazing out the back window of the general's jeep.

Back at headquarters, Major Hanson and the colonel were walking around the building with a hot dog and a pistol, calling sweetly, "Here, Schroder!"

The Box

I was alone in the aid-station when Sergeant Goodwin came in. The rest of the medics were sleeping while I pulled CQ and read "Atlas Shrugged." Outside, another monsoon shower spattered on the clay street. Goodwin stood at the door for a moment or two, letting the water drip from his fatigues and then he came over to the table where I sat. Under his arm, he carried a shoebox.

I started to ask him what brought him out in the middle of the night, but somehow I sensed that the question would be answered shortly, so I simply nodded at him, laid my book aside and waited for him to begin the conversation.

He sat the box on the table between us and quietly, almost reverently, he said, "Go ahead, Doc. Open it up."

I reached out and picked up the box. It felt empty. But when I lifted the lid and looked inside, my eyes fell upon a pair of human ears, laid out carefully on some tissue.

"These look pretty fresh," I murmured. The callousness of my remark shocked me and I felt a tinge of guilt as I set the box back down on the table.

"They ought to look fresh. I just lifted them last night. Pick one up, Doc. Feels soft as a baby's behind," he offered.

I don't know why I did it. Maybe I wanted to show him I wasn't squeamish. I'll never know exactly why, but I picked one of the ears up. It was soft, mousy soft, but very cold. I held the ear up to the light for a moment or two and studied the flap of skin where it had been separated from a man's head. The cut was clean - sharp knife.

"What are you going to do with them?" I asked casually as I lay the ear back in the box.

"Well, Doc. There's a young lady back in Kentucky who just wrote me a "Dear John" letter last week. I thought maybe I'd send her a little surprise package to express my displeasure about the situation," he said.

"You sound a little bitter," I noted.

His voice hardened. His jaw twitched as he answered, "Damn right, I'm bitter. You think maybe I shouldn't be?"

He didn't wait for an answer, but continued. "Let me tell you a little bit about this deal, Doc. Six months ago, life was sweet. Had a part-time job, a student deferment and a girl who said she'd love me forever. I was going to be a teacher, maybe a good one. But not now. I lost my deferment. No money. No connections - 1-A on the draft list. And now, I'm an eleven-bravo. One, one, bullet stopper. And my mind's become a cesspool, Doc."

He pointed at the box and whispered emphatically, "It's reduced me to that!"

I nodded to let him know I understood his feelings and let him continue on.

"We were down near Ben Phuc last night, watching a trail junction just east of the ville. 'Bout midnight, I heard movement, so I punched the others and woke 'em up. We had this plan, see? We were gonna do it the old-fashioned way, man. No frags, no 16's. Just a good, sharp knife."

He lit a cigarette, inhaled deeply, and leaned back in his chair. Then he went on.

"There was just this one gook. A perfect setup. We waited until the guy was right on top of us and then we took 'i'm. I clapped my hand around his mouth and Tripp hit him low. It was supposed to be a silent move. Quiet death, right?" he said.

"Right," I answered.

"Well, it didn't work out that way, Doc. Hollywood is full of it. Nobody dies quietly Doc. The gook almost bit through my hand."

He held his hand out to reveal several angry red, welts. I nodded my sympathy and the tale continued.

"Things got a little crazy at that point. Tripp and I were tryin' to stab the guy through a windmill of flailin' arms. He took a long time to die, Doc. And he didn't go quietly."

Then he appeared to change the subject.

"You remember Tim Donaldson?" he asked.

"The chubby kid that was a medic for Alpha Company?" I offered.

"The same," he agreed. "I was in his squad before I transferred to Recon. He was my best friend. Well, anyway, I was with him when he got zapped. The man was just tryin' to help somebody, Doc. Went to treat a wounded gook and the man had a hand frag hidden under him. Pieces and parts went everywhere. You know, I still don't know if we got all the right pieces in Tim's body bag. We may have left some of him laying in the paddy with what was left of the gook."

He snuffed his smoke out, promptly lit another and started again.

"Well, Doc, every time I lifted my blade last night, I thought of Donaldson and how he got it. I just couldn't stab the man enough to cool my rage. So, after it was finally over, I gave the gook a nice trim job. The rest of the guys were looking for gold, or money. But all I wanted was my pound of flesh."

Goodwin pointed at the box and for a moment, there was silence. Then he exhaled deeply and finished his story.

"Hey, man, tonight the whole thing hit me. I saw the gook's wallet laying on Jefferson's bed and I picked it up. Know what was inside? Pictures. Pictures of a woman and two kids. His family, Doc. And what did they sacrifice him for? For some political idea? Will they have it any better if we leave and they win? I doubt it. I killed a man and mutilated him. For what? Didn't do Tim Donaldson no good. And you know what? It won't do me no good to mail pieces of him to Kentucky."

Then he stood up and started for the door, but stopped before he opened it. "Thanks for lettin' me talk to ya, Doc. You really helped me. And by the way, you can keep the box."

Skis

In August of 1969, the 5th/60th went into Cambodia. It was neutral territory and we weren't supposed to be there, but intelligence had detected a large enemy force near the border of Vietnam and so we crossed the invisible line that separated the two countries.

The entire battalion was involved, which meant that the colonel moved his entire staff from the firebase out to the site of the action. A medical team needed to accompany them, so Captain Henderson, Jim Bonner and I went along. We packed a large supply of medical equipment and flew out with Delta Company aboard a Chinook.

It was not a pleasant journey. The Chinook was a very large helicopter, with blades fore and aft. It tended to wallow around in the sky and when loaded to capacity, it was very slow compared to a slick. The interior of the Chinook was dark, there was no slip-stream to refresh your mind, no open doorway to watch where you're going. There was nothing but the dark, the stench of fifty sweaty men and the pungent fumes of fuel being burned.

When we finally landed and the rear ramp dropped, I walked out into a soft rain falling on the most desolate area I had ever seen. The land was pockmarked with bomb craters and defoliant had been sprayed on all the surrounding vegetation. Looking west, toward the enemy sanctuary, there was no plant life, just an endless sea of mud and the stumps of dead trees.

The colonel's CP Tent was the only shelter in the area and it was there to keep the radios, medical supplies and officers dry. The rest of us were left to fend for ourselves.

Jim and I scrounged some metal fence posts from a local Green Beret outfit and built ourselves a lean-to. Our effort looked pretty good at first, but as the slicks began shuttling troops in and out of the area, we discovered a major flaw in our construction. The backwash from the helicopter rotors kept blowing our ponchos off the top of our shelter. It was nightfall before the lifts stopped and we could finally crawl under a roof, out of the rain.

Actually, we were very fortunate to have a roof. The rest of the men slept on the open plain. They had neither the time, nor the inclination to build anything. When the slicks wheeled in and dropped them off, they simply walked a few yards from the landing zone and collapsed into the thick, oozing mud. Soaked to the skin and weary beyond words, they silently curled up· in their ponchos with their weapons and slept with the rain falling into their faces.

Sometime during the night, a late arrival came in and half our roof disappeared. It was my half. Jim managed to grab his part, pulled it around him and went right back to sleep. I was left out in the proverbial cold, so I headed for the CP Tent.

When I got there, the place was crowded with officers planning the next day's operation. And I knew that the tent was off-limits to me, but I was determined to find someplace, anyplace that was dry, so I could get some sleep. It took me awhile to find an empty space in the crowded tent, but I finally spotted one. It was under the colonel's map table. I dropped down on all fours and crawled around until I worked my way to the desired location.

With my mission accomplished, I pulled my wet poncho liner around me and fell sound asleep, until a muddy boot hit me in the face. When I pushed the boot away, its owner bent over and I was face to face with Major Hanson, who demanded to know what I was doing there and simultaneously ordered me to get out. Before I could answer, or make a move to leave, the colonel came to my rescue.

"Leave the Doc be, Hanson. He ain't in our way down there. Let 'i'm sleep,"

I grinned at the major and nodded off.

The next morning I ambled back to our wanna-be lean-to and found Jim still sleeping between the empty posts. The rain had stopped and bright sunshine warmed the bones. With a little effort, I was able to get Jim out of his poncho cocoon and we fixed ourselves a hearty breakfast of mystery meat warmed over a lump of C-4. Then we went to search for my poncho/shelter-half, which we found about fifty yards away on the bank of a river.

By mid-morning, we had devised a much better shelter and had just finished it up when the first lifts of the day started coming in. Word spread quickly that there had been a major conflict early that morning when two of our companies, in conjunction with the Green Beret unit, had caught a large enemy unit with their pants down. Literally.

It seems that they actually assaulted an enemy base camp. The NVA unit was busy doing laundry and cooking breakfast when our troops jumped them. In the resulting fight, we ran up a body count that made our colonel the envy of every battalion commander in Vietnam. And to make matters even better, we captured a huge stockpile of enemy weapons and other assorted equipment.

Jim and I found no wounded aboard the incoming flights. All casualties had been sent straight to Third Field Hospital in Saigon. We went to work with the rest of the men, helping to unload the booty. It created a huge pile beside the CP Tent, where the colonel stood gloating over his treasure. To him, it was a gift from heaven. A reward for his diligent effort and the fruit of his labor.

To the grunts who had actually taken the prize, it represented nothing more than a pile of goods wrestled from those they had killed, and the sacrifice of the men who had died to get it. There was no joy glowing on their faces and no thrill of victory shining on their countenances. I saw only a deep look of weariness about them as they silently deposited their loads and moved slowly away to rest.

A sense of shame came over me as I watched the scene unfold. I felt like an intruder, a voyeur watching something I had no right to see. I knew how the line troops felt. I had been there. But I wasn't there anymore. And I knew instinctively that I was no longer a member of that fraternity. Membership there was expensive and exclusive. Once you left the line, you no longer qualified.

When the cache was unloaded, I went back to the river for some time to myself. I was on my third cigarette when I heard someone approaching. It was Jim.

"Wanna talk about it?" he asked.

"Not much to discuss," I stated. Then I began to vent my feelings.

We ended up talking for a long time. I shared my frustration and pain. Jim gave me reasons for hope.

Near the end of our discussion, the earth began to tremble as if an earthquake was striking nearby. Then a low, distant rumble rolled in and off to the west, wisps of dust and smoke drifted into the sky. The brass called it rolling thunder, the press called them B-52 raids. Thousands of tons of bombs were falling on our enemies.

As we stood watching the action, a new sound drew our attention back to the river. It was the roar of an approaching swift boat moving at full speed. We glanced in the direction of the sound and caught sight of the boat as it rounded a bend. In the bow of the boat, behind a set of twin fifty-caliber machine guns, stood a man in a swim suit and sunglasses. He was holding a beer. Further back, the pilot, too, had a Bud in his grip.

We watched them bore down on us, dumbfounded by the sight of them and then the weirdest part of all. Round the bend came a man on a slalom ski. He flashed past us in an instant, throwing up a huge rooster-tail and wearing nothing but a smile. With one hand he held the tow rope, in the other his beer.

When the boat disappeared from view, Jim sat down and lit up a smoke.

"You ski?" he asked.

"Not slalom," I answered.

No Body

It was raining in Rach Kien the night they brought him in. During the monsoons, it seemed like it was always raining, but that night in particular, the rain came down in sheets, turning the clay streets of the firebase into the consistency of Jello. We were watching "Star Trek" on our tiny television when the jeep he was in pulled up outside the aid-station. Major Hanson, the battalion XO (executive officer) was the first man through the door, then came two Vietnamese interpreters carrying his body wrapped in a blanket.

Without a word, the major motioned the two Vietnamese to deposit the body on one of our stretchers, then he turned toward me and asked, "Who's in charge here?"

Jim Bonner quickly stepped forward, "I am, sir. Specialist Jim Bonner."

"Well Bonner, I've got a little job for you to do this evening," the major began. "This man was the colonel's personal tiger scout and he was killed in the village tonight. The colonel wants a complete autopsy report down at battalion ASAP (as soon as possible)."

Bonner stepped over and opened the blanket to look at the body. We all looked at the body. The man was dead. Completely dead. On a scale of one to ten, he garnered every available point. He was burned beyond recognition. Both arms were blown off above the elbow and one leg was pretty much missing, too.

Bonner looked at the major, then back at the body, then back to major again, "You're kidding. Right?" he asked.

Major Hanson's face bore a slight smirk. He nodded his head and said rather stiffly, "The colonel doesn't joke about such important matters. Now he wants that autopsy and he wants it tonight. Understand?"

"Yes, sir!" Bonner snapped back.

The major turned on his heels and headed for the door with the two Vietnamese right behind him. He stopped in the doorway long enough to tell us that to the best of his knowledge, a hand frag had been involved in the incident. Then he vanished into the rain.

Bonner looked around at the rest of us with this incredulous expression on his face. He walked back over to the body and he just stood there for a minute. Then he pushed his glasses back on his nose and shrugged his shoulders. He spoke to no one in particular and so softly, it was hard to hear his voice above the pelting rain. "The man plays with a hand frag and it goes off. He's dead. Where's the mystery?"

Then he looked over at Sam and said, "Walters, go down to the officer's club and get Captain Henderson. We'll need him to do this job."

Bonner went to a storage locker for a surgical kit and the rest of us sat down to watch "Wild, Wild West," which had just come on the television.

When Captain Henderson came in, he and Bonner did the autopsy while the rest of us watched with mild interest. The doctor was all business as he moved from one end of the corpse to the other, pushing metal probes here and there, muttering to himself. It was an emotionless procedure that reminded me of two biology students dissecting a frog, probing the tissue before them, exploring the mysteries of anatomy.

Half an hour later, the autopsy was finished and Weird John typed up an official- looking document which Captain Henderson signed before he went back to the officer's club. Sam, who was still wet from his previous trip, delivered the document to battalion and the rest of us went back to our TV programs.

When "Wild, Wild West" went off, Bob Jennings suddenly jumped out of his chair and blurted out, "Jeez, this is givin' me the willies. Can't we do somethin' with that body?"

The rest of us just laughed at him. The presence of a corpse, just five feet away seemed perfectly natural. I mean, what's the deal?

"Look," he reiterated, "It's really buggin' me, OK? Let's put him somewhere!"

It was at that moment that Sam came back in. "The colonel liked our work. Seemed real impressed," he stated as he collapsed into a chair.

Bonner handed Sam a Coke and asked him if the colonel gave him any instructions about what to do with the body.

"Nope," Sam uttered between sips.

For a moment or two, Bonner stood staring at the blanket covered body. Then he threw up his hands and nodded to Weird John and me. "You two take Luke the Gook outside and put him in Wilson's jeep. We'll figure out what to do with him in the morning."

John and I removed the body unceremoniously. Other than Bonner, who held the door, no one else looked up from the television.

I was surprised by the weight of the man. He was typically small and missing several body parts, but still, he was heavy. When we reached Wilson's jeep, we couldn't maneuver the stretcher properly to get it all in the vehicle. For several minutes, we fumbled around in the pouring rain and then tiring of our futile effort, we just slid the body off the stretcher and let it crumple into the back of the jeep.

When we got back inside, the party was breaking up. The Armed Forces Network was signing off the air and one by one, we drifted out of the aid-station and into our barracks next door. As I lay on my bunk that night, I kept thinking about the corpse. No remorse or anything, just the nagging problem of what to do with him before he ripened. I mentally reviewed several options and felt that the problem was solved. However, I hadn't taken into account the actions of Harold Wilson.

Wilson was an alcoholic. At one time, he had been a platoon medic for Alpha Company. But one night he got careless and a man died. So he ended up driving a re-supply truck to Tan An twice a week and drinking the rest of the time.

Late on the night of our autopsy, Wilson came staggering up the street from the NCO Club. At some point, he made a decision to leave Rach Kien and his failure far behind. He found his jeep sitting beside the aid-station, and unaware of his extra passenger, he drove the jeep right through the western gate of the firebase and out into the countryside beyond.

Bonner, who was on CQ that night, called battalion and they sent out a platoon from Delta Company to search for Wilson. I remember standing in the doorway of our barracks and watching the men from Delta file by in the rain and mud. They were supposed to be standing down and they were not overjoyed at being called out in the middle of the night to search for a drunk.

It took them about an hour to find Wilson and the jeep. When they brought them to the aid-station, the only thing in the back of the jeep was Wilson, wrapped tightly in the blanket that had held our corpse.

"Where's the body that was in the back of the jeep?" I asked the Delta platoon sergeant.

The exasperated grunt just shrugged his shoulders. "Look, Doc," he offered, "When we found your buddy, he was sprawled in a ditch with the blanket over him. That's all there was. We didn't see no body."

Shoes

The firebase was always teeming with children. They were mostly young boys, who came in daily from the ville. The boys did odd jobs to earn a little cash, or more often than not, some cans of C-rations. Anything they could do, we didn't have to. So we let them shine our boots, sweep out our barracks and run errands for us. It was a win-win situation and besides, the presence of their smiling, dirty, little faces made things more bearable, less harsh.

I don't think anyone ever learned any of their real names. We simply called them George, or Bob, or most usually, just Boy-San and we sorted them out by the way they dressed, or by physical ailments that made them stand out from the others.

The Boy-Sans were regular customers at the aid-station. None of them owned a pair of shoes and they were continuously injuring their feet. I learned to suture on a little boy who had laid his foot open on a piece of broken glass. The boys were seldom hurt seriously, but due to the nature of our business, the possibility always existed that something serious could happen. On July 16th, it did.

I was working morning sick call, putting heating pads on boils and handing out aspirin, when a man from the Charlie Company mortar platoon came bursting in the aid-station.

"We need some medics down at the mortar pit!" he shouted.

Sam and I grabbed our aid-bags and ran after him to the accident site. When we got there, we found several men tearing at the wreckage of a collapsed house.

A sergeant who was directing the operation, told us what had happened.

"We were tearing down the house to make room for a new mortar pit and the house caved in on us," he stated. Then he pointed at the collapsed building and added, "There's a Boy-San under there somewhere. He was pulling loose wall boards off when the place fell in."

One look at the debris told me that Boy-San wasn't likely to survive. The roof of the house was laying flat against the floor.

We had to remove several sections of the roof before we found the boy. He was dead. His frail little body was totally crushed. We rushed him back to the aid-station and went through the motions of resuscitation, but we all knew it was a wasted effort. We were fresh out of miracles and his sheet-draped body ended up in the back of my jeep with his bare feet protruding.

While Sam went to battalion to find out what we were supposed to do with Boy-San, I sat out behind the aid-station watching over him. I didn't want him to be alone, and besides, the whole situation was eating at me. I mean, death was far too common in my life. It was an everyday occurrence. But it was usually another man and his passing often went unnoticed by anyone except his closet friends. The death of a child was different. It was the war's cruelest tragedy and I never got used to it.

My mind went numb as I sat staring at the boy's feet. They were so small, so scarred, so dirty. The kid needed some shoes.

I was still sitting out back when an interpreter from battalion arrived. He asked me to drive him and Boy-San home. It wasn't a job I particularly wanted, but it had to be done, and besides, the boy was in my jeep.

I will never forget the emotions churning within me as I drove slowly out of the firebase and through the village of Rach Kien. Even the activity in the marketplace ceased when I passed by. The people knew what I was carrying.

When we crossed the iron bridge just south of the village, the interpreter pointed to a hooch which squatted on the river bank. I eased the jeep to a halt and sat staring into the sky while my companion walked down a narrow path to Boy-San's home. He returned a few minutes later with a sobbing, young woman and an old man who stood by quietly as the sheet was lifted to view the body.

I couldn't look at the woman. All I could do was stare into space and fumble with the junk I had shoved under the driver's seat.

When the sheet was pulled back to expose the child's face, there was a strained silence. Then the woman let out a piercing scream that shook my soul. She went limp and the interpreter had to catch her. I grabbed an ammonia ampul from my kit and waved it slowly under the woman's nose to bring her back around. She moaned softly and began a quiet sob.

Then the old man and Momma-San nodded to us. They turned and headed back down the path. For a moment or two, I stood numbly in the roadway, watching the pitiful scene. Then the interpreter sighed heavily and said, "We need to take Boy-San home now. Please help me with the stretcher."

I lifted one end of the litter and as we began sliding it off the back of the jeep, my eyes fell on a pair of slip-on tennis shoes of mine that I had shoved behind the driver's seat. Without even thinking, I snatched them up and placed them on the stretcher. The kid needed some shoes.

Papa-San's Thumb

It was early afternoon when a pedicab brought Papa-San to us. I met him at the front door and helped him to a vacant stretcher. He was an old man, a very old farmer with a flowing white beard and a back bent permanently by his years in the paddies. His hand was wrapped in a blood-soaked rag and his face was etched with pain. Papa-San didn't make a sound, but sat stoically as his daughter explained what happened to him.

She told our interpreter that her father had gotten his hand caught in a piece of machinery, which severed his thumb. When I unwrapped his hand, he was definitely missing a thumb, but it was easy to see that a piece of machinery didn't do the work. His hand had no scratches on it - not even a bruise. And the thumb had been removed cleanly, almost like a surgeon had done it.

Captain Henderson asked me to clean the stump and numb it up so he could close the wound. As I did, he sat talking to the old man's daughter. He asked her what really happened and threatened not to treat the man if she didn't tell the truth. The young woman began to cry and begged us not to turn them away. She swore to our interpreter that there was no deception; her father had merely gotten a little careless. Her story didn't change.

The old man never spoke at all, but winced as I went about my labor.

There was no point in arguing with them. Nothing would be gained. So we sewed the old man up and gave him some pain pills and Tetracycline. Then he and his daughter went outside to sit and wait for the pedicab to return. That's when the discussion started.

Weird John was first to speak, "Papa-San got caught in the middle. That's what this deal is. If he doesn't wise up, he's gonna run out of digits."

Sam, who was watching Momma-San clean up, added his assessment, "Better a finger or two than his head. Decapitation is like total commitment, ya know?"

For a minute or two no one spoke and then Paul Davis summed it all up, saying what we all knew to be true. "It's a hell of a mess with no end in sight. That's what it is. A thousand years of brutality and these poor people got no way out. I mean, we tramp through his village by day, kicking over his water pots and burning his hooch because he shields the VC. Then they come in at night and chop off a finger or two because he was a little too cooperative. What really gets me is that we can't change it. We sew 'em up and send 'em back."

He paused a minute, then posed a question. "Now tell me this, gentleman. Who loses more? The man without a thumb? The man who took it? Or those of us that close the wounds?"

"We all lose," I offered. "There ain't no winners in this God-forsaken place. Anyways, I guess I'll see that Papa-San gets home OK."

I stepped outside the aid-station and sat down on a bench with Papa-San and his daughter. They smiled and bowed to me. I offered the old man a cigarette, which he gratefully accepted and for several minutes we sat smoking in silence. The young woman stroked her father's hair.

I kept looking at the old man's hand and I wanted to talk to him. I wanted to tell him that I was sorry we were all caught up in a senseless struggle. I wanted him to know that I saw his plight and if it were up to me, he could live in peace, till the soil and watch his rice dry in the sun. I wanted him to know that politics and fortune had thrown us together and that I knew a good day for him was two bowls of rice. A great day was three. But I realized that there was more than just a language barrier between us, so I sat in silence.

When the pedicab returned, I helped Papa-San get in, then I climbed into the back of the cab with the daughter and we rode the two clicks south to their village. The sun was low in the sky when we reached our destination. My patient and the girl were clearly uncomfortable with my presence and they tried to get me to just stay in the cab.

I thought they were just concerned for my safety - it wasn't a good idea to be on the road in the dark. But I gestured to let them know I wanted to help and we left the cab by the roadside as I helped them walk the last few yards home.

When we reached the old man's hooch, I understood their uneasiness and it wasn't the hour of the day that caused it. For there, nailed to the doorpost, was Papa-San's thumb.

The Sweepers

It was in late October when Steve Johnson caught a load of shrapnel and ended up in the Third Field Hospital. At home in Tennessee, the brilliant fall foliage was displaying itself in the crisp autumn air and the land was taking long drinks from gentle showers. But in Vietnam, the air was hot, dry and filled with metal.

Two days after Steve was dusted off, I hitched a ride up to Saigon and stepped into a different world. The hospital compound had an atmosphere of quiet solitude and the buildings were all painted a glistening white. Covered walkways connected everything and flower gardens bloomed in little courtyards. It was a little different from the dust and stench of Rocky Kilo. Made me feel uncivilized.

The wonder of it all confused me and I got lost while trying to find Steve's ward. For some time, I wandered here and there enjoying the pleasant surroundings. Then I rounded a corner and discovered something altogether different from the gardens. It was a large, paved courtyard, covered completely over by a roof. Several Vietnamese women were busy sweeping the pavement while another lady sprayed the area with a water hose. The women chattered as they worked and I stopped to watch them, fascinated with their routine.

Then hell on wheels arrived.

The sound of approaching sirens filled the air and the sweepers quickly hustled onto the walkway where I stood. Three army ambulances skidded to a halt beneath the canopy and at the same time, a side door to an adjacent building burst open and medical teams rushed out to meet the human carnage.

I realized in an instant that I had stumbled into a receiving area and I really didn't want to see what was unfolding before me, but I couldn't move. I stood rooted to the spot and watched mutely as the wounded were unloaded.

All told, there were about a dozen casualties brought in. The medical teams were a blur of activity as they jumped from one stretcher to another, sorting the wreckage. Uniforms were cut away and examinations carried out to determine which of the wounded would receive treatment first. Those who could be saved were treated first, the rest were left to themselves. Triage is a cruel business.

The whole scene was one of incredible gore. Blood ran freely from the stretchers and dripped onto the pavement where it mixed with the water and created a crimson sea. The medical teams kicked up red rooster tails as they scurried among the men.

Actually, "men" is a term loosely applied. The wounded were all very young and they looked more like a high school football team than soldiers. But the team was horribly transformed and athletics was something most of them could only look back on, not participate in. There were a lot of missing limbs.

The closest stretcher was only a few feet away from me. It was occupied by a young, blonde-headed soldier. He lay writhing and twisting, his face a mask of pain. He was covered with mud and his tears left little white trails as they rolled down his cheeks. In the midst of the noise and confusion, I heard him call hoarsely for his mother. A nurse who was standing nearby heard him, too, and she stepped over to take his hand. Then she gently brushed back his golden curls and bent down to whisper in his ear.

The young man became very quiet and still. He sighed and closed his eyes for the last time. The nurse looked up at me and our eyes locked. She was crying.

When she placed his hand back on the stretcher and reached down to pull a sheet over him, my mind went back to Ben Luc and I could see Charlie Sheppard disappearing beneath his poncho liner.

I forced myself to move on and for quite a while I wandered aimlessly, not caring where I went. Eventually, I did find the orthopedic ward where Steve was recovering and we spent some time together enjoying a final visit. Steve had a million dollar wound - he was on his way home. You couldn't see my wounds, there was no treatment for them and I was going back to the delta. We parted with promises to look one another up someday back in the world. A promise neither kept.

On my way out, I tried to by-pass the outdoor receiving area. I didn't want to be there when another load of wounded arrived. But I didn't know where it was, nor how to avoid it. So I ended up right back in the courtyard where the ladies were still cleaning. Almost involuntarily, I stopped once again to watch them. Water splashed, the brooms swished and the momma sans spoke in hushed voices.

As I stood watching them, I began to wonder. How many times a day does this place need cleaning? How many men have passed through this fearful portal? What price does this place really extract?

The questions seemingly had no answer. But then I realized that I was looking at the only ones who could truly answer me. And a voice within whispered, "Ask the sweepers."

Connie's

Connie's served food and beverages. But it wasn't a restaurant or a bar. It was an army mess hall and its official name was actually Con-4. The name denoted the fact that it was an army kitchen and that it served four battalions of men all their meals. The name, "Connie's," had been lovingly bestowed on the facility by some unknown soldier on whom history had played a cruel trick - he had to eat in the place.

I became acquainted with Connie's and her legions of army cooks in 1967 while in training at Ft. Devens, Massachusetts. Connie's was a sprawling H-shaped edifice containing one enormous kitchen in the center of four large dining halls, which formed the wings. Each dining hall had its own entrance and along the outside wall, a tunnel-like shelter had been constructed so the troops could line up for chow out of the weather.

The interior walls of the tunnels were covered with every sort of graffiti imaginable, a virtual smorgasbord of the English language. The names, addresses and phone numbers of half the female population of the United States appeared there, along with little bits of wisdom and vulgarity. As we waited in line to get our meals, we had an unlimited supply of reading material and each day new quotes appeared to pique our interest.

Of all the human thoughts recorded there, only one remained in my memory when I left Ft. Devens. I found the quote on my first visit to Connie's, halfway down a tunnel, at eye level. You would be hard pressed to miss the words. They were scrawled in large, red letters, and proclaimed boldly, "Halfway around the world, at the sewer of the universe, a toilet sits. Above this porcelain disposal, a sign hangs which says - Flush twice, it's a long way to Connie's."

It usually took a new arrival only one visit to confirm the truth of those immortal words.

Two years after leaving Ft. Devens, I was in Saigon. After visiting a wounded friend at the Third Field Hospital, I flagged down a pedi-cab and took a wild ride across the city to the USO. The food there was excellent and I made short work of the first hamburger and French fries I had tasted in eight months.

After my meal, I shot a few games of pool and then, as luck would have it, nature called. I went to the men's room to relieve myself. When I stood up to flush the commode, I happened to glance at the wall behind the toilet. There, penned neatly in red letters was the inscription, "Flush twice, it's a long way to Connie's."

I chuckled quietly as I waited for the tank to fill again and then I saluted as I flushed the second time.

Terminal Illness

Every Tuesday was medcap day for the battalion aid-station. It was always the same routine, it never varied. After breakfast, Ron Johnson, Rick Tobias and I would back a 3/4 ton truck up to our metal storage shed and load the truck with medical supplies. Then we'd swing by battalion headquarters to pick up two interpreters and our assignment for the day. Another Tuesday, another little village filled with the sick and infirm. It was, at best, a somewhat boring routine. The idea of helping others had worn thin. We just wanted to survive our 365 days and go home.

Tobias drove the truck, Ron served as navigator and I rode in the back of the truck with the two interpreters. The ride out was always exciting, as we attempted new speed records with each run. The interpreters would hold on for dear life as we careened through the countryside and I clung to an M-60 machine gun mounted to the bed of the truck. I don't know why I stood behind the gun. I didn't know how to operate it and besides, it was never loaded. The ammo was stored in boxes, which bounced around amidst the other supplies as we ran the roads.

We were like a bunch of kids playing with whatever was at hand and we made the most of every opportunity. But on a Tuesday afternoon in November, it all changed and med-cap day took on a new meaning for us.

We were visiting a village named Phu Bai. As usual, we borrowed some tables from the local people and set up shop. One of the interpreters circulated through the village to announce our arrival and attempt to gather some intelligence. The other one stayed with us so we could communicate with the people.

It didn't take long for a large crowd to gather. They filled the central marketplace of the village and crowded around our tables to watch us examine each patient, laughing and jabbering as we handed out little cardboard boxes of multi-colored pills. They jockeyed for the best position to see everything that went on.

To us, it was merely business as usual. To them, we were like a mobile Mayo Clinic.

Halfway through the morning, a young mother showed up with her twin sons. Both of the babies had boils covering their heads.

Ron looked at me in exasperation when he saw them and said, "I don't think I'll ever get used to this."

Then he motioned toward the truck and muttered, "Go get a couple of sheets. It's surgery time for the boilsy twins."

When I got back with the sheets, we wrapped the little boys up from the neck down to keep them from thrashing around and settled down to work. First, we washed their heads down with hydrogen peroxide and then, one boil at a time, we sprayed a freezing compound on it to deaden the area. The skin turned white, and little crystals of frost sparkled in the sunlight.

Once the area was numbed, a scalpel was used to lance the boil and remove the core. Then we packed the boil with sterile gauze and applied an antiseptic bandage. It took almost an hour to complete the job and during the entire time, the two babies screamed at the tops of their lungs. We were bathed in sweat and our ears were ringing.

When we handed the twins back to their mother, Ron told her, through the interpreter, to bring the babies into the aid-station every other day to have the bandages changed. Then he looked at me and said wryly, "We'll never see them again, but what can we do?"

After the surgery, we needed a break, so we went to a nearby soup stand and ate Chinese noodles, which we washed down with coke. While we ate, the rest of the village took their daily siesta to escape the blazing sun. The marketplace was empty, until an attractive young woman carrying a plastic tote bag came along. We watched her closely as she circled our treatment tables and Rick remarked, "I hope that one comes back when we re-open for business. She obviously needs a complete physical."

We finished our lunch to the rhythm of her swaying hips and watched her disappear when the crowd started to gather up again.

Our first patient of the afternoon was an old man who drooled betel nut juice.

"Haw," he said and then he gave us a fairly convincing cough to prove his point.

The interpreter fought back a grin and said, "Sir, this man has a very bad cough. He needs something to soothe his throat."

I gave the interpreter a wink and passed him a bottle of ETH with codeine. "Tell him to take two teaspoons every four hours, and no more." Then I turned to Rick and said, "One bottle, plus one beer equals dreamland." We laughed together and the line moved on.

The next hour or so was fairly routine. As Solomon said, "There's nothing new under the sun." We poked, prodded and pushed pills to an endless array of peasants as their friends and neighbors watched with interest. At one point, I caught sight of the young woman with her tote bag and told Rick to get his stethoscope ready, but when I looked back to where she stood, she was gone.

It was late in the afternoon when I saw her again, moving through the outskirts of the crowd and little by little the people began to thin out. I should have realized that something was up, but a born optimist is easy to blind-side. At one point, she came close to our tables, but a group of children crowded in and she moved away into the center of the marketplace.

A few minutes later, an old woman gathered the children up and scolded them. Then the young siren started back toward us, her pink silk top flowing around her.

I remember watching her approach. Her movements were graceful and demurring. I remember looking at her face and how beautiful it was. And I remember how the sun cast little lines of light on her cheeks through her straw hat.

Something inside my brain kept trying to tell me that she had fatal intentions and that she carried her tote for an express purpose. But her beauty short-circuited my alarm system and I could only watch as she moved closer. I turned to Rick, who was equally spellbound and as I did, there was a terrific explosion.

Instinctively, I dove beneath the table in front of me and when I looked up again, the woman lay crumpled in a pool of blood in the center of the marketplace. Her legs were gone.

For a moment, there was only stillness and then a flurry of motion as the villagers simply evaporated. The torso of our siren lay twitching in the sunlight.

Ron was the first to move. Then Rick and I followed him over to check the young woman, though there was little doubt as to her disposition. As we stood over her lifeless body, Rick nudged her with his boot. Then he gave me a nervous grin and remarked, "We can't help this one at all. She obviously had a terminal illness."

Moon Gold

Under normal circumstances, there are a certain number of people who exhibit behavior that most of us would call weird. These people don't usually do anything dangerous and, by and large, folks don't think that much about them. However, Vietnam was not even remotely close to normal life and somehow that changed things when it came to eccentricities.

For instance, we had approximately 1200 men in our battalion at any given time. Among that number, one would expect to find maybe a handful of weirdos. Not so. When eminent danger, high explosives and stressed-out men are thrown together as we were, the weird count grows exponentially.

It seemed that some deranged grunt was always doing something totally strange, mostly stupid and often deadly. When that happened, the man's entire outfit suddenly didn't know the man. They would basically go into hiding and call the medics to deal with him.

We had our fair share of twisted individuals during my tour, but I met the craziest of them all, the crème de la crème of weirdness on Halloween night.

I was on CQ that night and was rather pleased that it had been a quiet evening. There had been no interruptions of a Monopoly game, which had been in progress since 6:00 p.m. It was a dog-eat-dog financial free-for-all with no holds barred. By 11:00 p.m., Weird John was bankrupt and sat sipping beer while Jim Bonner and Ron Johnson were hammering out the details of a mortgage deal that would keep Jim in the game. I was flush at the time and sat listening with amusement as my two remaining opponents harangued each other.

Then the front screen door fairly burst open and a wild-eyed grunt from Charlie Company rushed into the room. "We need some medics out at the front gate ASAP!" he said breathlessly.

Jim looked over his property cards at the man and asked, "What's the problem? Somebody get hurt out there?"

"Not yet, Doc, but Grover's on the loose. Anything could happen. He's trick-or-treating."

Somehow, the significance of the reported event was lost on the rest of us and for a second or two, we just looked at the man. Then it occurred to me that no one normally ran into the aid-station in the middle of the night unless something was wrong. So I quickly folded my Parker Brothers cash and pushed it in my breast pocket. My property cards got shoved into my jungle pants. Regardless of where the night's activities took us, I wasn't about to lose my comfortable advantage. I owned Boardwalk and Park Place.

"Maybe you should give us a few quick details," I interjected. "What's going on out at the front gate?"

The man heaved an exasperated sigh and said hoarsely, "Grover Washington is out trick-or-treating, Doc!"

"So?" I remarked.

"So he ain't wearin' no costume." He returned.

"How shocking," Jim snorted. "An obvious breach of seasonal practices."

"And a tasteless holiday faux pas," observed John.

"He ain't got no mask, either," giggled our guest.

"Well," I remarked, "Just what is the problem? We need details!"

"Ok. Ok." He began. "We were out on the berm tonight on guard duty. Somebody pointed out that it was Halloween. So we started tellin' ghost stories and a few of us had a joint or two. Well, one thing lead to another and before long, Grover decided to trick-or-treat the hooches outside the north perimeter. Since he didn't have no costume, he just jerked his fatigues off and headed out stark naked. All he's got, besides his dog tags, is his cigarette lighter and a hand frag. Now you understand?"

"Great!" moaned Jim.

The grunt offered an apology. "We tried to stop him, Doc. Honest we did. But Grover is a big dude and he just ran away from us!"

Ron rolled his eyes as he looked at me and said, "Well, you're

CQ. Who's gonna play trick-or-treat with Grover?"

It was obvious to me that Weird John wasn't going to be any help, so I nodded at Jim and Ron. "I guess we're elected," I muttered. Then I asked Weird John if he could handle the phone in case battalion called.

"I'm fine," he said thickly. "I can handle anything. No problem."

I wasn't all that confident in John's answer, but under the circumstances, I didn't have much choice. So we grabbed some sheets out of a storage locker and took an ambulance out to the main gate, where several men were milling around.

"Which way did he go?" Jim asked as the ambulance coasted to a stop.

Before anyone could answer, a woman's piercing scream split the air and as we turned to look in the direction from which it came, a fire broke out on the roof of a hooch about a hundred yards to our left.

"He's right down there, Doc," someone laughed. "And it looks like they didn't have no treats for Grover!"

"Well, that's just dandy!" Ron hissed. "The colonel will be right in the middle of this one!"

"Look," I ordered the nearest man. "You ring up battalion and tell them we're out on the perimeter. Then call your mortar platoon and get some illumination up. And some of you guys get down there and put the fire out! We'll take care of Grover."

"Gotcha covered, Doc," he shouted after us, as we ran into the night armed with only our sterile bed linens.

A couple of minutes after our departure, parachute flares began floating softly to earth and everything took on a peculiar orange glow that was in keeping with the holiday. The scene was one of complete confusion. Three of us were flitting from house to house through the shadows calling Grover's name. The local population was wailing and moaning as though the devil himself had gotten loose among them and Grover's drugged buddies were conducting a Chinese fire drill.

Grover was the only man out that night that knew what he

doing. And he was stoned.

Try as we might, he stayed just beyond our grasp, cackling and snarling at us. Then he called out in a booming voice, "The moon is full of gold!" and we got a fix on his position.

"What now?" I asked Jim.

"No problem," he answered confidently. "You go around to the front of the hooch and get his attention. Distract him with your charm. Then Ron and I will tackle him from behind."

"Well, that sounds simple enough," I retorted. "But how come I have to go eyeball to eyeball with this lunatic?"

"Look," Jim answered, "This guy is rather large, right? So, since Ron and I are big too, we'll do the physical part. You just get his attention. Then we'll hit him from behind."

"Suppose he decides to pitch his hand frag," I countered.

"Then Ron and I will see that he rots in jail," Jim returned

"How comforting," I spat as I walked away.

I slowly worked my way around to the front corner of the hooch. Then I peeked around to see where the guy was. But the front side of the hooch was in deep shadows and I couldn't see a thing. With a sigh of resignation, I edged around the corner, and then, practically at my feet, a deep voice boomed, "Boo!"

It was Grover Washington, squatting on the ground.

My mouth flew open and I tried to yell, but all I managed to do was suck in a chestful of air. I jumped backwards and sat on the ground.

Grover just laughed and said wildly, "The moon, the moon is full of gold!"

I couldn't speak. My eyes were riveted to the hand frag he was holding.

For several seconds, we just looked at each other, and then I found my voice.

"I know, man. You found any nuggets?"

"Oh yeah," he giggled. Then he held out the grenade and whispered, "Look at the size of this one!"

"The mother lode!" I exclaimed. "You've found the Mother Lode! Hey man, can I hold it?"

"You promise to give it back?" he whimpered.

"Oh sure," I answered. "You found it, didn't you?"

We both stood up and slowly he stepped toward me. Gingerly, he held out the object, and when my hand closed around it, I realized that it wasn't a hand frag, after all. It was just a smoke grenade.

I was so relieved, that I began to laugh.

Then Ron and Jim hit him from behind and in a flash, the naked trick-or-treater was bound from head to toe in sheets.

"The frag! Where's the frag?" Jim shouted.

He pointed to me and asked, "What is that?"

I didn't hesitate an instant. I just pulled the pin and dropped the smoke grenade at his feet. There was a soft hiss and then bright yellow smoke billowed around us.

"It's moon gold!" I answered.

Merry Christmas

It was Christmas Eve and the aid-station was ready for the holiday. Red, gold and blue ornaments hung from the ceiling of the treatment room, along with streamers of silver. Ron Johnson and I made a large banner that read, "Merry Christmas and Happy New Year - Peace and Goodwill to All Men," which we hung outside the front door. We had a small, artificial, Christmas tree, which Paul Francis had brought down from Saigon. It stood in one corner of the treatment room with brightly wrapped, but empty packages spread beneath it.

We did what we could to summon the spirit of the season, but admittedly, it didn't seem much like Christmas. The dead and dying came to our door daily, even though we were supposed to be observing a truce. Every night, the artillery battery had firing missions, and out in the countryside, our units still had LP's posted to keep tabs on the enemy. Besides, if it was Christmas, where was the snow?

In spite of it all, late in the evening, the celebrating began in earnest. Most of the medics, myself included, were hanging around the aid-station. Whenever the rest of the men decided to celebrate, they got careless. And when they got careless, somebody generally got hurt. We had to pick up the pieces, so the medics celebrated in shifts.

It was shortly after eight o'clock when we heard someone singing, "Deck the halls with boughs of holly, 'tis the season to be jolly!" The front door burst open and in staggered a black man in a Santa suit. It was Captain Fuller from the intelligence section and he was clearly in a holiday mood.

"How ya'll doin'?" he asked, and then, without waiting for a reply, he continued on. "It's totally cool at the North Pole, man, and I just want you men to know that I'm havin' a hell of a time here in Nam. You ever try to land a sleigh in a rice paddy? Messy. It's very messy. My reindeer are up to their antlers in mud. I'll probably have to get an APC (armored personnel carrier) to pull me out!"

He then produced a bottle of Jack Daniels, took a long pull, and then offered the bottle to Rick Tobias. We passed the bottle until it was empty and everyone was feeling mellow. Then Santa decided it was time to get our Christmas wishes.

"This ain't Macy's," he said, "But as long as I've got this job, all God's children get to tell the Soul Santa what they want for Christmas."

One at a time, we sat in Soul Santa's lap and divulged our deepest desires. We became starry-eyed children.

When the wishes were all expressed, Soul Santa produced another bottle, which he finished himself, and then he passed out. His mission was accomplished. We laid him on one of our stretchers and most of the rest of us were ready to call it a day, when a truckload of carolers pulled up outside the aid-station. "I'm Dreaming of a White Christmas," echoed softly in the night.

We stepped outside to receive our well-wishers and to my surprise, I found most of my old platoon in the back of the truck. The last line of their song died away, and then, Purple Hayes, who was driving the truck, shouted to me, "Hey, Doc, we came to get you, man. We're celebratin' third herd style. Get in and let's go carolin'!"

With a little help from my friends, I clambered into the back of the truck and we drove off into the starry night. Around and around the compound the truck circled while we sang, "Joy To The World," "Little Town Of Bethlehem," and every other Christmas carol in the book. The words were jumbled, we sang off-key, and the choir was a mixed bag of the human race, but our hearts were in unison.

After several turns around the firebase, we stopped in front of battalion headquarters, where we began shouting for the colonel. He came out in his underwear and to our surprise, he joined in as we sang joyously to the Prince of Peace. Fortunately, he didn't ask where we got the truck.

When we finished our repertoire of carols for the colonel, he wished us all a Merry Christmas and Hayes drove the truck down to the artillery battery. We parked the truck and went into their EM Club to continue the celebration. Our relations with the artillery boys were always cordial, but not exactly friendly. Sometimes they screwed up and when that happened, it made life interesting, if not deadly.

But on that night, things were different. The holiday spirit reigned over all of us and we were one big happy family. One by one, each man was hoisted atop the bar and a toast to our health was consumed. When I found myself standing above the others, I was declared, "the best damn medic in Vietnam and an angel of mercy, to boot." I cried with joy.

The party lasted far into the night, until the bottled spirits were gone and our own spirits were full. The last toast of the evening was reserved for those we had lost. It was as though they were there with us, hovering over our gathering. When I lifted my final glass, I gazed into the rafters and I saw their faces, smiling peacefully at our poor effort to honor them.

The party ended and we loaded everyone in the truck. Out on the wire, another Christmas celebration began. Every bunker on the perimeter opened up and a thousand tracers shot into the sky. Flares and illumination rounds filled the night. It was Christmas morning and we expressed our joy in the only way we knew.

When I got back to the aid-station, I walked in to a scene of wild confusion. Some local folks had brought a young woman in to have her baby and she was in heavy labor. The expectant mother was screaming and moaning. An older woman, who I guessed to be her mother, was bathing her forehead and crying. An old man sat nearby, chanting softly. Paul Francis and Dr. Henderson were trying their best to help, but there was little they could do - except wait.

I was in no condition to help anybody, so I collapsed into a vacant chair to watch the miracle of birth. On the stretcher next to the young woman, Soul Santa was still snoozing, his exhaled breath stirring his artificial whiskers.

It was just before dawn when the baby came. First the head crowned and then with all the strength she had left, the young woman thrust the child into the world. It was a baby boy. He came as all of us do, covered with a cheesy coating and the blood of his mother. The old man danced with joy and grandma clapped her hands softly. The new mother smiled weakly and the rest of us broke into broad grins, completely caught up in the advent of life.

As I watched Paul gently bathe the new baby and wrap him in a soft cloth, my mind whirled far away and long ago to a little town in Judea where another baby boy had come in much the same way. It gave me hope.

In the midst of our miracle, Soul Santa suddenly came to. He rubbed his eyes to clear his vision, then he sat straight up and shouted at the top of his lungs, "Merry Christmas!"

Welcome Home

In the early morning light, a nudge and a familiar voice awakened me. It was Ron Johnson and his words were music to my ears. "Wake up, short-timer, it's time to go back to the world."

I rolled over to face him, a smile playing on my lips. "Say it again, Ron. It sounds so good!"

He grinned at me and turned away, then he shot back over his shoulder, "Let's go down to the mess hall for breakfast. It's your last chance to get a case of the trots here in beautiful Rocky Kilo!"

"I'd rather eat C's, thank you!" I called back as he disappeared through the screen door. It was the morning of March 1, 1970. My last day with the 5th/60th.

I lay for a few minutes staring at the ceiling. There was no reason to hurry. All my packing was done and I had no duties to perform that day. I wanted to savor the moment. Let it sink in. I pushed my poncho liner off and lay naked, letting the breeze from the ceiling fan stir me to life. Ron's words echoed in my mind, "It's time to go back to the world."

Then apprehension set in. Questions flooded my mind. For sure, I wanted to leave. I'd had a bellyful of Vietnam. But I wasn't sure that I could go home and if I did, who would I be when I got there? I did know that the man who had arrived a year earlier no longer existed. So who was I? The name was the same, and the social security number would be the same. But there the likeness ended.

I looked down at my nakedness and laughed out loud. The first thing I would have to do would be to learn to put on underwear again. Then other questions invaded my thoughts. How could I ever fit in again? I had become accustomed to violence and mayhem. The steady cadence of artillery firing lulled me to sleep every night. Coarse gestures, bad language and canned food were my daily fare. Sudden death was my norm.

I was comfortably uncomfortable and the world I was returning to was quiet, well-mannered and frightening.

With a sigh of resignation, I pulled on a pair of cut-offs and headed for the shower house. Outside, the sun was blazing away and a slight breeze stirred the dusty street. Heavy black smoke swirled into the air behind our latrine and the pungent odor of burning excrement wafted in the wind.

After my shower, I stood behind the shower house and gazed out across the north perimeter of Rach Kien. It looked exactly like it did the first day I arrived. Rolls of wire, trip flares and claymore mines were interspersed among the tombs and bunkers. But unlike my first view of the killing ground, my last look was different. There were no longer any questions in my mind regarding its sinister purpose and it commanded my attention only because a deep sadness weighed upon me as my eyes swept its plain.

The sound of an approaching pedicab caught my attention and I made my way back to the aid-station to see what the morning had brought us. I arrived just in time to hold the door while the patient was unloaded - a small boy, covered in blood. Two old men carried him in and a young woman, who I guessed to be his mother, followed behind them sobbing and wailing.

In spite of the fact that I was officially off duty, I jumped in with several others to do what I could. We cut his ragged clothes away and discovered multiple shrapnel wounds covering his frail body.

Paul Francis, who was in command at the time, looked at me as we sponged the blood away and said grimly, "Looks like you get one last heartbreak."

I returned his gaze and nodded in agreement. There was no need to answer him. We both knew that the boy would die.

Captain Henderson came in as we finished cleaning the wounds. He took one look at the boy and grabbed a trach kit from a wall locker. There was little conversation on our part, each of us knew what to do as we worked feverishly against the odds. I grabbed a bottle of D5-W from a shelf and hung it up while

Paul worked to find a vein that hadn't collapsed.

While we were starting the IV, Jim Bonner and Captain Henderson were busy doing a tracheotomy. Tobias was busy bandaging the wounds and Weird John was on the horn calling for a priority dust-off.

It took only a matter of minutes for us to complete our work. The boy was cleaned and bandaged, his IV was running at full tilt and the trach tube was taped securely in place. I sat down in a chair and closed my eyes. Detachment was absolutely necessary. In the background, I could hear the voice of the interpreter sorting the mess out. The boy had tripped a booby trap while playing near his village. Right. It was always the same story with predictable results.

"ETA on the bird is seven minutes. They want red smoke!" Weird John's terse words snapped me back to action and I took my place at the head of the stretcher, ready to hold the IV bottle as we transported our patient. Tobias took the front handles and Ron Johnson lifted the back and we headed for the helipad with me carrying the IV and Paul walking along beside the boy. Momma-San walked behind us, still wailing.

Halfway to our destination, the boy began to suffocate again. His breakfast was oozing from the trach tube. Without hesitation, Paul pulled a short section of rubber tubing from his breast pocket and orally suctioned the food out of the airway. My stomach churned as I watched him spit the half digested food on the ground. But Paul's quick thinking did the trick and the boy relaxed and began to breathe again.

We reached the helipad just as the dust-off came into view. Red smoke swirled around us as we loaded the boy and his mother for their ride out. Then Paul shouted something to the dust-off medic and I noted that he merely shrugged his shoulders as the slick lifted off.

We backed away and for a moment I stood frozen, watching my last medi-vac soar away. Then I turned and found Paul retching his own breakfast. When he finished, I offered the towel that was still draped around my neck and he wiped his face. Paul looked at me through tired eyes and muttered softly, "They don't have a suction pump on the slick. The kid will choke to death any minute now."

I spent the rest of the morning hanging around the aid-station, watching the others conduct daily sick call and occasionally lending a hand. Weird John suggested a trip to Harry's Bar, but I declined the invitation. "I think I'll stay right here, John," I told him. "This is my briar patch."

"OK, man," he answered. "But this ain't Uncle Remus, even if you do look like Brer Rabbit."

It was eleven-thirty and I had just finished packing a boil, when Ron stuck his head through the front door and called out, "Last bus for the Freedom Bird is now boarding! All short-timers load up!"

When I turned toward the door, I found a line of smiling faces waiting to bid me farewell. Sam and John, Jim and Paul stood waiting for my exit. For me, it was an awkward situation. A typical male scenario. No hugs, no words of endearment. Just a firm handshake and a, "See you back in the world."

Outside, I found my gear already loaded in the jeep and beside it stood Momma-San.
Her large body was trembling and there were tears in her eyes. With her, there was no protocol. She had washed my laundry, shined my boots and mopped up blood with me. Almost every day, she had brought fresh melons from her garden. She was, indeed, my Momma-San. We stood for several minutes together with our arms around each other.

Then I sprang into the jeep and Ron started for the front gate, down the dusty avenue. I turned back for one last look and there stood Momma-San, waving her shawl to me. I waved back, and as I did so, we turned the corner. She was gone.

The trip out was like a stroll down memory lane - nothing had changed since the day I had arrived full of questions and apprehension. The schoolhouse by the front gate was full of smiling children who waved as we passed. Up the road, a small Catholic church stood serenely nestled in its garden and a priest who was at the front gate, bowed to us as we passed. Then we crossed the iron bridge with its bunkers and beyond that for several miles, there was nothing but rice paddies and lines of nipa palms. My eyes constantly scanned the nipa. It was a habit.

When we reached the intersection of Highway 4, Ron pulled in to Susie's Place. "Let's have one for the road," he suggested.

"For sure. One for the road," I answered.

We found Susie curled up in the lap of her latest lover, but when we stepped onto the veranda, she jumped up to offer us service. "You number one," she told us. "You want cold beer? Cold coke? You like hot soup? My soup number one!"

Ron looked at me and winked. "Everything with Susie is number one. Ever notice that?"

Then he turned to Susie and said, "Fix us some soup, Susie. And two cold cokes. My buddy here is going home. He needs a good meal to get him started."

Susie flashed a big smile. "For sure, bouxi? You go home?" she asked.

"Yes Susie. I'm going home," I answered.

"Lunch free today!" she laughed.

We sat in the shade for some time, eating slowly and watching the traffic stream by. Neither of us spoke much, I suppose because neither of us knew what to say. Ron and I had become close friends and spent a lot of time together, but I suppose we both realized that the kinship was based on the violent world into which we had been thrust. It wasn't the real world, the world to which we would return. And I guess at the bottom of it all was the certain knowledge that we would never see each other again after that day. There was no need to increase the strain with a sad good-bye.

Once the meal was gone and Susie had hugged me farewell, we merged into the flow of traffic heading north toward Saigon. Once again, I found myself caught up in an endless throng of soldiers, peddlers, peasants and prostitutes, all moving in the tide of life. It was a time of remembrance for me and I sat as if in a trance.

My mind went back to the day Ed Garcia was killed. I could feel the force of those terrible explosions when the AK opened up on him. I could see his crumpled form lying on the trail and taste the rich, earthy mud that coated my face. Then I remembered how soft the rain felt falling on me, the mist that swirled around in the jungle, and Ed disappeared in the fog.

Charlie Sheppard materialized. For the hundredth time, I relived the night he died and all my inadequacies welled up again. If I had moved faster, or been better prepared, could I have saved him? If I could have found a vein and gotten the IV going, would it have made a difference? Lt. Gray said nothing I could have done would have mattered. But it wasn't his job to save Charlie. It was mine, and I couldn't do it.

I was lost in a vortex of violence as other incidences began to haunt me and then Ron's voice broke through. "Hey, man, you with me or what?"

"Sorry, Ron," I offered, "I was just remembering some things."

Ron must have guessed where I'd been, because he looked over at me and said, "Don't think about it too much, buddy. And don't visit the dead. For you, it's over and you can't change anything. Mind games can be dangerous."

On the outskirts of Saigon, we passed the coke stand where Wayne had donated the contents of his buddy's wallet to the young pimp. She was still there, hawking cokes and her sister. I waved as we passed by and she smiled broadly, motioning for us to stop.

Then we entered Saigon with its' hordes of beggars and thieves. The crowded streets slowed our progress as we wound north through the city heading for the 90th Replacement Battalion where I would process out. When the main gate at Long Binh came into view, a 707 passed overhead and I smiled broadly as I watched it gain altitude. I looked over at Ron, and he, too, was watching the plane.

After we were cleared at the gate, we drove slowly down the access road that wound its way through the base. Scattered along the way were the same shanties, garbage piles and ragged children I had seen a year earlier - nothing had changed.

When we reached the building marked "Returnees," Ron coasted to a stop. We sat for several minutes, neither of us speaking. Then Ron silently swung his legs out of the jeep and began unloading my gear. I jumped out to help and when everything was piled on the ground, I took his hand for the last time, shook it warmly and said, "Thanks for the lift, friend."

Ron looked at me and a broad grin suddenly broke across his face. "You beat the odds, you know that?" he asked. "You pulled it off, man. You're goin' back to the world!" Then he jumped back in the jeep and as he started to pull away, he shouted back over his shoulder, "I'm sixty-one days behind you!"

"See you back in the world!" I returned as I watched the jeep retreat down the dusty road and Ron disappeared in a cloud of red dust.

When I stepped inside the building, I found a lone clerk lounging beneath a ceiling fan. His feet were propped up on his desk and he was reading a paperback novel. As I dropped my papers on the counter, he looked over his book and asked, "When's your DEROS?"

"Tomorrow," I answered.

He grunted and laid his book down. Then he came over to look at my orders and after a quick scan, he reviewed the list of no-no's for returning GI's. Nobody with VD. No drugs, no weapons and no offensive photographs.

I shook my head, giving a negative reply to each question. But in the back of my mind, another series of questions lurked. Questions the army didn't ask. Questions they didn't want to know the answers to.

When my record review was over, the clerk told me where to catch a ride the next morning. Then he pointed to some nearby barracks and said, "You can stay over there tonight. Take any empty rack you can find." He returned to his story and I went to find a place to sleep for the night.

The barracks reminded me of Ft. Lewis, sparsely furnished with cast-off bunks and in dire need of a good cleaning. There were several other returnees who had already moved in, but they were strangers to me. Other than a nodded greeting, none of us communicated with the others. I unrolled my mattress, dusted it off and piled my gear on the floor. Then I wandered off to find the EM Club. I was in limbo again, belonging to no one. I felt detached and useless.

I spent the afternoon at the EM Club and had a hamburger for supper. Then I headed back to my barracks. Out on the berm, close to my quarters, a group of new guys were watching a gunship work the north side of the base. I stopped momentarily and my mind flashed back to the time I stood where they were, spellbound by the symmetry of death. For just an instant, it entered my mind that I should go over and talk to them. Maybe tell them that the beauty they were seeing was sinister and deadly. And for sure, there wasn't any glory that could be associated with it.

I had this urge to grab them by their collars and tell them the truth. But then I realized that there was no way to get through to them. It was a vain hope. They would have to find out for themselves what was really going on out in the bush. And Vietnam was a good teacher. They would feel the heat and the fear. They would see the gore, smell the stench and in the end, possess the bitterness.

When I entered my barracks, they were still standing on the berm hooting and cheering.

In the late night hours, a siren sounded and I awoke. For a moment or two, I lay listening to the wailing and strained my ears to catch the sound of the impacting rounds. They weren't falling anywhere nearby, so I decided not to move. Outside, the new guys were running around beneath the glow of illumination and shouting, "Incoming!"

The guy in the bunk next to me rolled over and asked me, "You goin' anywhere, Doc?"

"Home tomorrow," I answered and I went back to sleep.

I spent my last morning in Vietnam hanging around a small PX (Post Exchange) near my barracks, where I bought a camera and a watch to take home with me. As I was walking back to gather up my gear, someone shouted my name. For a second or two I didn't realize they were talking to me. I had become accustomed to "Doc." Nothing else rang a bell. Then the voice called again and I looked across the street to see a familiar face.

It was Tim Boyd, a guy I had gone to high school with. He stood waving wildly, a big smile on his face and a new uniform on his frame.

"I can't believe this," Tim remarked. "What's the odds of two guys from Lawrenceburg, Tennessee, meeting here?"

"Life is crazy!" I laughed.

Tim took note of my faded fatigues and pointed to the medic's patch above my breast pocket. "It looks like you've been here a while. Seen much action?"

"More than I wanted to," I answered.

"Where you goin' now?" He asked.

"Home, Tim," I said. "I'm goin' home."

"I'm goin' to the 25th Division. You know anything about them? I mean, where are they? Is it bad there?"

"You're goin' northeast, Tim. They operate in a place called the Iron Triangle. I don't know anything about the area, but if it's in Vietnam, it's not good."

He shrugged at my reply and the conversation turned to other matters. I saw a wedding band on his left hand and asked who the lucky girl was.

"Denise Brewer, you remember her?" he answered. "She was a junior when we graduated. Lived up around Ethridge."

I nodded and he continued.

"She didn't want to wait. I got drafted and she said there was no sense in putting it off."

"So, how long you been married?" I asked.

"Six months and most of the time I was in training. She came down to Ft. Gordon while I was in AIT (Advanced Individual Training). Got to see her on weekend passes. She's home with her parents now. Would you give her a call when you get home? Maybe tell her that I'm OK and that there's nothing to worry about?"

I agreed to lie for him and we talked for a few more minutes. Then I noticed a truck parked near my barracks. I realized that my ride to Ton Sonute was waiting. I gave Tim a final handshake and told him, "I've got a plane to catch. Listen, Tim, don't do anything stupid. Keep your head down. I'll see you back in the world."

He smiled and nodded. "You don't have to worry about that, man. I've got a little lady waiting for me. I'm only 361 days behind you!"

I left Tim standing in the dusty street at Long Binh and three weeks later he was killed in action. No one from Lawrenceburg ever saw him alive again.

It was a short, sweet ride to Ton Sonute and I soon found myself standing beneath the same open terminal I had visited a year earlier. Nothing had changed, there were still large groups of new men warily eyeing the rest of us. I looked around to see if I recognized anyone, but saw only strangers. So I started counting the new faces and applied my Bravo Company casualty rate. The numbers got so depressing, that after five minutes, I had to quit. I dozed off in the hot, still air.

"You goin' back to the world, or you gonna stay here in paradise?" The joking question and a boot nudge woke me up. I looked up to see a captain in faded fatigues smiling down at me.

I stood up, shook his hand and told him, "I'm saddled up, sir. Let's di-di-mou."

We joined the other troops lining up to leave and after a clerk checked our names off the manifest, we made our way onto the tarmac where a 707 stood waiting for us. There was no pomp or ceremony. No fond farewells. Just a long line of strangers straggling up a ramp to catch their ride out of the inferno.

As we entered the cabin, a pretty stewardess with an antiseptic smile greeted each of us. The interior of the plane was sterile and cool. Soft music was playing on the intercom. It all seemed so foreign that I felt uncomfortable. I moved down the aisle and managed to get a window seat. It was incredibly plush by my standards and I sank down into it with a satisfied smile. Then I stared out the window across the airbase.

Heat waves radiated off the runway obscuring my view, but what my eyes could not see, my heart envisioned. I knew that beyond the runway lay wire and mines and scorched earth. And further still, lay the paddies and the villages of the Vietnamese people. I knew I was leaving all that I could not see behind, but there was no sense of accomplishment and no joy. Just a haunting emptiness and the certain knowledge that I had not contributed to any improvements. The war would continue. People would die and only the land would endure.

The seat next to mine gained an occupant and I turned to see the same cook that had left Seattle with me. We congratulated each other and sat making small talk until the "fasten seatbelt" sign came on. Then the atmosphere changed abruptly and the cabin fell silent. A knot formed in my stomach as we taxied out to the end of the runway. There was a momentary pause. The planes engines screamed. And then the plane surged forward.

When our wheels left the runway, the silence ended and every man on the flight cheered as we screamed into the sky. The soil of Vietnam no longer held our bodies, just our souls.

When we reached cruising altitude, the stewardesses moved among us, distributing reading material and soft drinks. They looked like Barbie dolls with soft, white skin and they smelled like Chanel No. 5. Other than a muttered, "Thank you, ma'am," or "No thanks," I didn't speak to them at all. How do you strike up a conversation with anyone, especially an attractive woman, when your only frame of reference is a day in the Eagle's Beak?

We landed in Japan to re-fuel and then flew straight on to Oakland. As the plane descended, I saw the Golden Gate Bridge shimmering in the morning sun. Its enormous towers cast shadows on the sea and the hills beyond lay in peaceful shades of deep green. Within moments our wheels touched down and another enormous cheer erupted from the passengers. When we walked down the ramp, the air was crisp and smelled strangely clean.

As we walked across the tarmac, voices shouting obscenities caught my attention and I looked at the fence near the terminal. A welcoming committee of several hundred protesters awaited us. They were marching up and down the fence line waving placards and slinging insults. When I neared the building, one of them called to me directly and said, "Hey, baby killer! Welcome home!"

Ghosts

He comes into my bedroom from time to time and just stands at the foot of my bed. He doesn't say anything. He doesn't need to. I know he's there and he knows that I'm aware of his presence. I'm just not sure why he's there. I do know that I'm awakened out of a sound sleep by the sound of his bare feet softly brushing my carpet. And then I sense that someone is staring at me. When he first began appearing, a sense of fear gripped me so strongly I could hardly force myself to look at him. But now, I'm resigned to the fact that he's there and rather than fear him, I just stare back. We look at each other in the darkness and sometimes I think there's some type of communication going on. But I can't be sure, because he's not a real person. He's a ghost. The ghost of a man I found lying in a wood line one night in the Mekong Delta.

His unit had blown an ambush on us. They had the element of surprise, but we had artillery. Within minutes of being pinned down by them, our fury screamed overhead and 155mm shells crashed into the jungle that concealed their unit. The air became filled with hot steel and the stench of burning nitrite. The trees splintered and the concussions hurt my ears. It was a time of terror. A time of death. A time to create ghosts.

When the barrage ended, we had to sweep through the wood line that separated the rice paddies. And that's when I found him. He was lying helpless and naked, except for his black, silk shorts. He was wounded, and my practiced eye told me, fatally. I had no way to find out who he was. The NVA didn't leave an ID behind when they abandoned their wounded. They stripped him and left him for dead. It was their way and the man understood it. He had no wallet, no pictures, nothing of a personal nature to keep him company during his final moments. There was nothing except this tiny, frail-looking, young man who lay beside a path through the jungle, with his blood soaking into the damp, rich, soil.

I remember that I took my foot and pushed him over to make sure he was unarmed. It was a foolish thing to do. I should have checked first to make sure he didn't roll off a grenade that was intended to send us both beyond the delta. But it had been a hard day and a harder night. I was weary and careless. Besides, he was mostly dead. I rolled him back over and I stood above him studying his face. His smooth, young face. It didn't register pain. Didn't show fear, anger, confusion, nor any other emotion that I could detect. We just looked at each other as he lay there, on that spot of earth, bleeding into his shorts.

Then his breathing ceased and his eyes closed. I checked his pulse. There wasn't one, so I left him there beneath the orange glow of the parachute flares and I moved on into the jungle to look for more of the enemy. At the time, I didn't feel anything, either. No compassion, no anger, no joy. Nothing. I felt nothing when I moved on into the night.

But the nights are different now. I feel things. And this slight, mysterious, young man keeps coming into my bedroom at night. He stands at the foot of my bed. He doesn't talk, but I think he wants to communicate. Maybe, since I found him, or since it was my artillery that killed him, he holds me responsible for his death. Maybe he wants an apology from me, or an explanation as to why I came home and he had to die. Maybe he wants to know why I lie next to my sleeping wife and his wife was left alone and weeping. Maybe I don't owe him anything. After all, he shot first - he just missed. We didn't.

I've finally decided that it's the way of war. Some are lost and some survive. Some heal and some are forever wounded. And some are ghosts, that keep coming into my bedroom at night.

In Focus

Sometimes the oddest things bring back memories of Vietnam. The wind for instance. The other day, I was out with my daughters at the neighborhood pool. Just myself and the three kids. It was about mid-day, hot and humid. The girls were splashing around, playing Marco Polo, and I was reading a book in the shade of a cabana. The wind started to gust, moving through the tops of the sycamore trees near the pool. I closed my eyes, listening to sound of the rustling leaves and in an instant, I was gone. The happy laughter of the children faded away and I found myself standing near a line of nipa, knee-deep in a flooded paddy. The sky was filled with huge, black, cumulus clouds and I could feel rain approaching in the wind that rustled the jungle canopy.

The dream was so real I could smell the rich, earthy odor of the paddy water. It was warm around my knees, but grew colder down around my ankles. My feet made funny, sucking noises as I sloshed across the paddy. All around me, men were shouting short, terse commands.

I glanced back over my shoulder and watched as seven helicopters rolled into the sky, gaining altitude and safety. A gunship appeared and began prepping the wood line with rockets and its mini-gun. My gaze shifted to the nipa again and I moved forward with the rest of the third platoon as we waded toward a paddy dike.

The gunship finished its work and rolled into the clouds. The wood line fell silent. One by one we clambered onto the paddy dike and began moving toward the point where the dike intersected a trail that disappeared into the nipa. We hadn't moved more than a couple of steps when Bob Edwards tripped a toe popper. He stepped out of the paddy and practically landed right on top of it.

I was looking at him when it happened and I watched with a mixture of horror and fascination as he sailed back into the paddy. There was a sort of muffled explosion, mud and water mushrooming all around him, and Bob flew upwards as if jerked by an invisible hand.

When he surfaced in the water, he started screaming for me, but I was already sprinting down the dike toward him. Two of his buddies jumped in to help him and by the time I reached them, they had dragged him out onto the dike. He was clutching his right knee and moaning, "Doc, do I still have a foot?"

"Yeah, Bob. It's still there," I assured him. What I didn't tell him was that he might not keep it. He was pretty mangled.

"You're gonna be alright, Bob. We're gonna fix you up and send you home. You'll be like new when I finish." I'm sure my words were comforting, or at least appreciated, but I was weary of lying to men like Bob. I was tired of pieces, parts and gore. And completely worn out by the responsibility of saving lives. Sometimes I couldn't.

I gave Bob a shot of morphine and wrapped him in his poncho liner. He passed out and the RTO called for a dust-off. Then we set up security and sat on the dike smoking while we waited for the medivac.

After Bob had been picked up, we moved on down the dike into the tree line. It seems odd now, but that was the way things happened in Vietnam. One minute a friend was there with you, held close by the bond of trust, and then in an instant, he was gone and you just moved on. Humping the paddies, carrying your load and losing pieces of yourself.

When we reached the edge of the trees, we found a crude sign tacked to a stump. "Tu Dai," was scrawled in large red letters.

I asked Song, our tiger scout, what the sign meant.

"Booby traps," he whispered. "Beaucoup VC here, Doc. This place number ten!"

Nervous laughter erupted ahead of us and someone said, "They should have posted the sign out on the dike."

Movement down the trail slowed to a snail's pace and it took more than an hour to pass through the jungle and out into the paddies beyond. As we reached them, we spread out on line, sweeping toward another nipa grove. It was exhausting work, wading through the thigh-deep water and pulling your feet out of the ankle-deep mud beneath it. A slow drizzle began to fall as we neared a dike in front of the trees. Firing broke out to our right. Someone had spotted movement in the trees.

We lunged forward and took cover behind the dike, waiting to see what developed. Then I heard an approaching helicopter and I rolled over on my back to see a cobra gunship appear above the jungle behind us. It looked like a giant grasshopper with pods of rockets bristling beneath its stubby wings and a mini-gun hung from its snout like a large, black cigar.

Black puffs of smoke erupted from beneath the gunship and in a heartbeat, several rockets whizzed just above us. They slammed into the trees just yards away and we were lifted out of the water with the force of their explosions.

"Pop smoke, damn it!" Lt. Gray yelled to the RTO.

Spider Dixon deftly pitched a smoke grenade over the dike and our position was quickly marked with purple smoke that settled over us in the heavy air. The gunship ceased firing and pulled up into the clouds. The firing to our right stopped and we moved on into the trees. An hour of searching in the semi-darkness of the jungle yielded nothing. It was just another day of sweeping tree lines and finding nothing.

Darkness was almost upon us as we reached another open paddy and the slicks swept in to pick us up. It was a dangerous time of day to be on the ground, so all we got was a quick hover. We jumped on and the paddies disappeared in the dusk.

As we rolled out over the darkened delta, I sat in silence listening to the sound of the ship's blades biting into the air. I shivered as the slip-stream moved across my wet uniform and I thought about Bob. I wondered if he would lose his foot and I wondered how much of me was lost that day.

"Daddy! Sissy won't give me my float!" A small voice startled me and I jumped slightly as I looked up to see my youngest daughter standing in front of me. She was pouting, but so beautiful and so alive. I pulled her into my lap and gave her a strong hug. The paddies faded away, the questions subsided and I was back in focus.

Circle Around The Sun

For those of us who survived it, Vietnam is a constantly evolving experience. It moves in and out of our lives on cat's feet, silently stalking our memories. These memories are precious. They were obtained at a great price. And they are as much a part of us as our right hands. Sometimes they bring joy, as we remember happy moments and younger days, when our backs were limber and our bellies were flat. Other times the memories are dark and brooding, as we recall deadly encounters and personal failure. What the memories never bring, is closure. For that, you need a wall.

In December of 1988, I made a visit to the Vietnam Veteran's Memorial in Washington D.C. It was there, in the presence of my family, that I came face to face with the things that I had kept bound up inside for so many years and I found a way to let them rest.

Our first stop was at the statue of the three grunts, which stands at the top of the hill overlooking the monument. The figures looked so life-like, that it hurt me to view them. It was as though all the men of Bravo Company were standing before me. They looked like they had just come in from the field. Even their eyes reflected weariness. I remember mumbling something incoherent and my wife squeezed my hand.

I gazed at her and said softly, "That's us. That's just how we looked."

Then we moved down the pathway, past the bookstands with their alphabetical listings of those who had fallen. At the time, I didn't even realize why the books were there. We stopped briefly at the near end of the memorial and I let my eyes run down its length. It was overwhelming. The polished stone glistened in the late evening light and the endless rows of names glowed golden from the sun's reflection.

I remember standing perfectly still for a long time and thinking, "My God, how many lives were wasted."

At first, I was afraid to begin moving down the face of my past. I didn't want to be reminded of the sacrifices I had witnessed. My children ran on ahead, unaware of the deep emotions tearing into my soul and it was actually me following them into the depths of my history.

We traveled the entire length of the stone, moving quietly among the many other visitors. Panel by panel, I viewed the names, occasionally stopping to read one. Now and again, I took note of the remembrances left at the memorial's base. It was a sobering experience, reminding me of how great a conflict Vietnam had actually been.

My daughters were awed by the memorial. I remember my oldest asking me, "Daddy, did all these people actually die in Vietnam?"

Unable to reply, I simply nodded in confirmation.

We returned to the listings and I noted the panels and lines where I could find my friends. One at a time, I visited them all.

My first stop had to be Ed Garcia, my old roommate. As I stood staring at his name, I could still hear him confess his fear and I was once again reminded of his true bravery. On the same panel, I found Bob Cole and Felipe´ Ramos. They had fallen together with Ed in the rain and the mist and now their names shone forever in the sun. James Taylor said it best, "They were true love, written in stone. They were never alone. They were never that far apart."

We moved on and I found Jon Robertson. As I paused before him, it was as though he was gazing back at me from the depths of the stone. I kept seeing him standing in the street at Rach Kien smiling bravely before he went out to die. In the midst of my thoughts, my middle daughter asked quietly if I knew the man well and how he died. I stifled my emotions momentarily, and tried to tell her how Jon had dashed from cover and fell from among us. But either she was too young, or the story was too old and she didn't understand.

Finally, she blurted out, "But why did he die?"

I remember kneeling beside her and brushing the hair out of

her face. Then I whispered to her, "Jon died because he loved his friends more than he loved himself. He tried to save their lives and it cost him his own."

"Sort of like Jesus?" she asked.

"Yes, dear," I answered reverently. "Sort of like Jesus."

At the end of the day, I went to see Charlie Sheppard, the man I couldn't save. In my mind, an apology was forming, but when I found him the words wouldn't come out. I simply stood before him and wept. Then I reached out to press my fingers into the letters that formed his name.

Behind me, I heard my daughter's tiny voice. "Did you know that man, Daddy? How did he die?"

I couldn't answer her. There were no words adequate to tell her the story.

I closed my eyes and pressed my fingers deeper into the stone. I was in the delta again. It was almost daybreak on the river. The only sounds were the muffled throbs of the boat's engine and water gurgling softly along the hull. I looked down into Charlie's face, and for the first time, I saw peace there. So I let go of his hand and watched him float away, like a circle around the sun.

From the story *Rocky Kilo*. The aid-station's grinning vulture.

The main street in the Rach Kien firebase. Note the large, black cloud in the center of the photo. The results of an airstrike nearby.

A typical rice paddy being planted by farmers. Note that all the people in the photo are women.

From the story *Soap*. The village elder gets his pills.

A lift of seven slicks comes in to take us out on a search and destroy mission. Note the dry rice paddy adjacent to the roadway/heli-pad.

The view from our "chariots." Note the large, dry paddies and the small patches of trees that gave the land a checkerboard appearance.

A sweep along the MeKong, April 1969.

Gary Pedone, aka "Coniglio" carries his M-79 on a sweep along the MeKong.

From the story *Fear*. The real Ed sits with his hair blowing in the slipstream.

From the story *Skis*. Sleeping quarters amidst the defoliated earth.

From the story *Skis*. Life in the rain and mud on the Cambodian border.

The author practicing field medicine on the Cambodian boarder.

From the story *In Focus*. The real Bob after his encounter with a toe-popper.

From the story *No Body*. Note the sawhorses and stretcher on the left side of photo where our corpse resided briefly.

From the story *Charlie*. This is the bunker on the BenLuc dredge where Charlie's accident occurred.